I0649584

also by Leslie Dick

Without Falling
Kicking

LESLIE DICK

The Skull of Charlotte Corday

and other stories

SCRIBNER

SCRIBNER
1230 Avenue of the Americas
New York, NY 10020

This book is a work of fiction. Names, characters,
places, and incidents either are products of the author's
imagination or are used fictitiously. Any resemblance
to actual events or locales or persons, living or dead,
is entirely coincidental.

Copyright © 1995 by Leslie Dick

All rights reserved, including the right of reproduction in
whole or in part in any form.

This collection was first published in Great Britain
by Martin Secker & Warburg Limited.

SCRIBNER and design are trademarks of
Simon & Schuster Inc.

Manufactured in the United States of America

1 3 5 7 9 10 8 6 4 2

Library of Congress Cataloging-in-Publication Data
Dick, Leslie, date.
The skull of Charlotte Corday, and other
stories / Leslie Dick.
p.   cm.
I. Title.
PS3554.I29S56   1997
813'.54—dc21   97-2204
CIP

ISBN 0-684-83439-1

Please see page 225 for text credits.

A woman's life is almost
devoid of syntax.

Viktor Shklovsky,
Zoo, or Letters Not About Love

Contents

The Skull of Charlotte Corday

Skull of Charlotte Corday (Fig. 1)

Dismembered limbs, a severed head, a hand cut off at the wrist . . .
feet which dance by themselves . . . all these have something peculiarly
uncanny about them, especially when, as in the last instance, they
prove capable of independent activity in addition. As we already know,
this kind of uncanniness springs from its proximity to the castration
complex. To some people the idea of being buried alive by mistake is
the most uncanny thing of all. And yet psychoanalysis has taught us
that this terrifying phantasy is only a transformation of another phantasy
which had originally nothing terrifying about it at all, but was qualified
by a certain lasciviousness — the phantasy, I mean, of intra-uterine
existence.[1]

One: 1889

Controversy at the Universal Exposition in Paris, on the centenary of the Revolution, as rival craniologists examine the skull
of Charlotte Corday, kindly loaned for exhibition by Prince
Roland Bonaparte, great-nephew of Napoleon and noted
anthropologist, botanist, and photographer.

Professor Lombroso, criminal anthropologist, insists (after a
brief examination of the skull) that specific cranial anomalies
are present, which confirm his theory of criminal types, or
'born criminals'. He subsequently uses three photographs of
the skull of Charlotte Corday, in his book *La Donna Delinquente,
la Prostituta e la Donna Normale* (Turin, 1893, co-written with
Guglielmo Ferrero, translated into English and published in
1895 as *The Female Offender*) to demonstrate that Corday, despite
the pure passion and noble motive of her crime, was herself a
born criminal, and therefore in some sense destined to murder:

3

Political criminals (female). — Not even the purest political crime, that which springs from passion, is exempt from the law which we have laid down. In the skull of Charlotte Corday herself, after a rapid inspection, I affirmed the presence of an extraordinary number of anomalies, and this opinion is confirmed not only by Topinard's very confused monograph, but still more by the photographs of the cranium which Prince R. Bonaparte presented to the writers, and which are reproduced in Figs. 1, 2, 3.

The cranium is platycephalic, a peculiarity which is rarer in the woman than in the man. To be noted also is a most remarkable jugular apophisis with strongly arched brows concave below, and confluent with the median line and beyond it. All the sutures are open, as in a young man aged from 23 to 25, and simple, especially the coronary suture.

The cranial capacity is 1,360 c.c., while the average among French women is 1,337; the shape is slightly dolichocephalic (77.7); and in the horizontal direction the zygomatic arch is visible only on the left — a clear instance of asymmetry. The insertion of the saggital process in the frontal bone is also asymmetrical, and there is a median occipital fossa. The crotaphitic lines are marked, as is also the top of the temples; the orbital cavities are enormous, especially the right one, which is lower than the left, as is indeed the whole right side of the face.

On both sides are pteroid wormian bones.

Measurements. — Even anthropometry here proves the existence of virile characteristics. The orbital area is 133 mm.q., while the average among Parisian women is 126. The height of the orbit is 35 mm., as against 33 in the normal Parisian.

The cephalic index is 77.5; zygomatic index 92.7; the facial angle of Camper, 85°; the nasal height, 50 (among Parisians 48); frontal breadth, 120 (among Parisian women 93.2).[2]

'The skull of Charlotte Corday herself' — Charlotte Corday, the 'angel of assassination', the beautiful virgin who fearlessly killed Marat in his bath, and calmly faced the guillotine, certain of the righteousness of her act. Corday becomes the paradigm of Lombroso's theory of innate criminality, simply because in every other respect she was so pure, so devoid of criminal characteristics. According to Lombroso, atavism in the male reveals itself in criminality; by contrast, the atavistic female is drawn to prostitution. Corday's virility is thus confirmed by her virginity.

The 'criminal type', or born criminal, is central to Lombroso's theory of anthropology. W. Douglas Morrison, Warden of H.M. Prison, Wandsworth, writes in his 1895 introduction to *The Female Offender*:

> The habitual criminal is a product, according to Dr Lombroso, of pathological and atavistic anomalies; he stands midway between the lunatic and the savage; and he represents a special type of the human race.[3]

Lombroso himself generalizes with ease about the female criminal type:

> In short, we may assert that if female born criminals are fewer in number than the males, they are often much more ferocious.
>
> What is the explanation? We have seen that the normal woman is naturally less sensitive to pain than a man, and compassion is the offspring of sensitiveness. If one be wanting, so will the other be.
>
> We also saw that women have many traits in common with children; that their moral sense is deficient; that they are revengeful, jealous, inclined to vengeances of a refined cruelty.
>
> In ordinary cases these defects are neutralized by piety, maternity, want of passion, sexual coldness, by weakness and an undeveloped intelligence. But when a morbid activity of the psychical centres intensifies the bad qualities of women, and induces them to seek relief in evil deeds; when piety and maternal sentiments are wanting, and in their place are strong passions and intensely erotic tendencies, much muscular strength and a superior intelligence for the conception and execution of evil, it is clear that the innocuous semi-criminal present in the normal woman must be transformed into a born criminal more terrible than any man.[4]

In 1889, as part of the Universal Exposition at Paris, numerous scientific congresses were held, and it was possible to attend three or four at a time. That summer, simultaneously there took place the International Congress of Physiological Psychology, the International Congress of Experimental and Therapeutic Hypnotism (participants included Freud, Myers, James, and Lombroso), and the Second International Congress of Criminal Anthropology. Many years later, Lombroso referred to that summer in Paris as that grievous or wretched time ('*dolorosa*'),[5] and this wretchedness was due, at least in part, to the violent arguments that took place between Lombroso and the French craniologists, notably Dr Paul Topinard, over the skull of Charlotte Corday. Lombroso recalled that the only truly happy moment of his stay in Paris was when he was permitted to examine the skull itself, which was entrusted to him by Prince Roland Bonaparte.

Lombroso was particularly thrilled to find, on the skull of Charlotte Corday, the median occipital fossa, upon which his theory of criminal atavism rested. Nineteen years before, in 1870, '*in un fredda e grigia mattina di dicembre*' — 'on a cold, grey December morning',[6] Lombroso performed an autopsy on the skull of Villella, a thief, and discovered this cranial anomaly, which he believed related directly to the skull formations of apes. Lombroso kept the skull of Villella in a glass case on his desk for the rest of his life, and in 1907, he wrote: '*Quel cranio fin da quel giorno divenne per me il totem, il feticcio dell'antropologia criminale.*' — 'From that day on, this skull became for me the totem, the fetish of criminal anthropology.'[7] It was the median occipital fossa that proved to be the bone of contention, so to speak, at the Second Congress.

Turning to *L'Anthropologie*, volume 1, 1890, we find, on the very first page of this first volume, the text referred to by Lombroso as 'Topinard's very confused monograph', entitled 'À propos du Crâne de Charlotte Corday'. In this work, Topinard implicitly criticizes Lombroso's techniques of measuring cranial anomalies, but more importantly, rejects Lombroso's interpretations of these measurements. Topinard insists there is no determining connection between the shape of the skull and the psychology or behaviour of the human being:

Our project is not to describe the skull as if it were that of a known person, with the objective of comparing craniological characteristics with the moral characteristics historically attributed to this person. We merely wish to take the opportunity for a study which could be carried out on any other skull, its object being to place before the eyes of our readers a summary of the manner in which, in our view, given the current state of the science, an isolated skull should be described, inspired by the methods and the very precise procedures of our illustrious and late lamented teacher, Paul Broca.[8]

Topinard goes on to emphasize the importance given by the school of Broca to averages, and therefore the relative insignificance of a single skull. On the other hand, he writes, with a very precious skull, it is correct to photograph and measure it, carefully, so that our grandchildren can make use of this data later, when science has progressed further. Topinard's description of the skull itself is vivid:

The skull, before my eyes, is yellow like dirty ivory; it is shiny, smooth, as, in a word, those skulls that have been neither buried in the bosom of the earth, nor exposed to the open air, but which have been prepared by maceration [soaking], then carefully placed and kept for a long time in a drawer of a cupboard, sheltered from atmospheric vicissitudes.[9]

Topinard goes on to emphasize that, above all, the skull is normal, symmetrical, 'without a trace of artificial or pathological deformation, without a trace of illness',[10] etc. It is the skull of a woman, 23 to 25 years old (Corday was 24 when guillotined), and there follow twenty-four pages of close technical description, eschewing any overt moral or sociological commentary. In conclusion, Topinard clearly disagrees with Lombroso:

It is a beautiful skull, regular, harmonic, having all the delicacy and the soft, but correct curves of feminine skulls.[11]

7

For Topinard, the crucial fact is that, quite apart from exhibiting the appropriate delicacy and softness of normal femininity, this skull is an average skull, typical of European females. Topinard admits there are a few minor asymmetries, but insists these are insignificant, merely 'individual variations'[12] on the norm. Topinard's polemic quietly but insistently defends Charlotte Corday's reputation, denying the virility, pathological asymetry, and abnormality attributed to her by Lombroso.

Ironically, on p. 382 of the 1890 volume of *L'Anthropologie*, Topinard is obliged to insert a belated Errata to his essay on the skull of Charlotte Corday. He notes that it is a rare exception that a text so full of numbers should appear without some errors of transcription or typography. He himself spotted one such error, and 'M. Lombroso' caught another. Nevertheless, he writes, these slight changes do not affect in any way the terms of his polemic. It is easy to imagine Lombroso's satisfaction upon discovering these slips.

Clearly, the disagreements between Lombroso and Topinard went deeper than techniques of measurement. Yet Lombroso, who was Jewish and a Dreyfusard, wrote a book on anti-Semitism in 1894. He was against nationalism, militarism, and colonialism, and was the very first socialist candidate elected to the town council of Turin in 1902. His research into pellagra, a skin disease that ravaged the peasant population, was controversial, but accurate, and he struggled for many years to have his findings recognized and acted upon. Nevertheless, Lombroso's primary scientific project of criminal anthropology depends on the construction of a hierarchy based on genetic characteristics, and on theories of atavism and degeneracy. (In 1892, Max Nordau dedicated his extremely influential and pernicious book on degeneracy to Lombroso.)

By contrast, Topinard, reviewing an anonymous polemic that proposed the forcible deportation of all seven million black Americans to Africa, in order to avoid racial disharmony, writes:

The solution is original, but impossible to realize . . . Instead of

8

indulging in such a utopia, wouldn't the anonymous author do better to say that if the black and white races do not mix in his country, this is due to the inveterate prejudice of the Americans, who create an intolerable situation for the blacks, pushing them into an isolation in which they can only see them [the whites] as the enemy, a class which humiliates them, abuses its intellectual advantages, and refuses them an equal chance in the struggle for existence.

There is only one significant fact in the state of things revealed by this book: this is that the blacks, in the United States, after twenty years of emancipation, remain pariahs . . . Here it is the question of the workers, the Jewish question, the Chinese question. The Negro question is of the same kind: anthropological notions of race have no bearing on it whatsoever.[13]

Lombroso's scientific socialism would probably have come under the heading of what Gramsci later dismissed as 'Lorianismo', after Loria, the political theorist whose most striking proposal was that everyone should have their own aeroplane, a utopian vision of Los Angeles freeway urbanism long before Los Angeles existed.[14] After a lifetime spent fascinated by the skulls of people of genius, political criminals, and anarchists, Lombroso became, in his later years, a fanatical spiritualist. His death, in 1909, was marked by obituaries on the front pages of daily newspapers in Russia, the United States, and Japan. The disposal of his corpse is noteworthy; Giorgio Colombo's recent book on the Museum of Criminal Anthropology in Turin, founded by Lombroso, includes a large photograph of Lombroso's head, beautifully preserved in alcohol in a glass jar. Colombo explains:

Among the papers of the illustrious professor, his family found three different wills, made at three different times, with small variations of a familiar kind. But one disposition, constant in all three wills, clearly indicated an explicit desire of Cesare Lombroso, which his relatives must strictly observe. This required that his body be taken to the laboratory of forensic medicine, to undergo an autopsy by his colleague Professor Carrara — this was to reply, *post mortem*, to those who had accused him of only working on the bodies of the poor. His skull was to be measured and classified, and then mounted on the rest of his skeleton; his brain was to be analysed in the light of his theory of the relation between genius and madness. Whether Carrara carried this out is not known; today the skeleton hangs in a glass case in the museum, the brain in a glass jar at its feet. In another case nearby stand the receptacles containing the intestines and the face itself. What remained of the body was cremated, and the ashes are to be found in an urn in the cemetery, between the painter Antonio Fontanesi and the poet Arturo Graf.[15]

The face of Cesare Lombroso in its jar, with his squashed and moustachioed features pressed against the glass, is a sight that, once seen, is not easily forgotten.

Two: 1927

Marie Bonaparte, also known as Her Royal Highness Princess Marie of Greece and Denmark, was the only child of Prince Roland Bonaparte, owner of the skull of Charlotte Corday. She was seven years old in 1889, and later vividly remembered the inauguration of the Eiffel Tower and the Universal Exposition. She remembered also the reception that was given by her father for Thomas Edison, a very large party that included among the guests a group of American Indians in war paint and feathers. A number of different nationalities appeared as ethnographic and anthropological displays at the Exposition, imported especially for the event, to be measured by the anthropologists, and photographed by Prince Roland.[16] The 'Peaux-Rouges', however, were represented in Paris by Buffalo Bill Cody's troupe of performers, Sioux Indians from Dakota, most of whom politely refused to allow the scientists to measure their heads and bodies. These were the guests at the Prince's reception, in honour of Edison as an American. Marie remembered asking her father for permission to attend the party, if only for a little while. He refused. She wrote to him: 'O Papa, cruel Papa! I am not an ordinary woman like Mimau and Gragra. I am the true daughter of your brain. I am interested in science as you are.'[17]

In 1923, during the long hours spent at her beloved father's bedside, as he battled with terminal cancer, Marie Bonaparte discovered Freud, through reading his *Introductory Lectures on Psychoanalysis*, which had just been published in French. As a child, Marie was particularly vulnerable to her father's frequent absences, prohibitions, and general unavailability, because her mother had died only a few days after giving birth to her. In the year of his final illness, Prince Roland could no longer leave her, and they spent every day together, taking lunch and

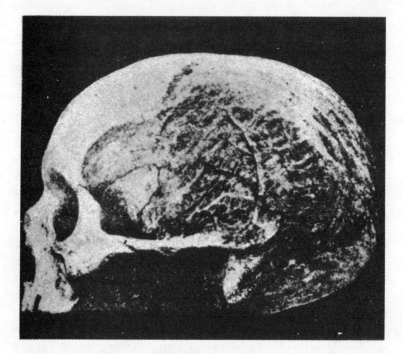

Skull of Charlotte Corday (Fig. 2)

dinner by themselves. Her father finally died in April 1924, the same month Marie Bonaparte's pseudonymous article on the clitoris appeared in the journal *Bruxelles Médical*.[18]

Marie Bonaparte was fascinated with the problem of female frigidity, a condition she herself suffered from, and her 1951 book *De la Sexualité de la Femme* (translated into English in 1953 as *Female Sexuality*) is reminiscent of Lombroso in its constant appeals to an ideal of normal femininity. In 1924, her article, 'Considerations on the Anatomical Causes of Frigidity in Women', argues that while certain types of frigidity are due to psychic inhibition, and are therefore susceptible to cure by psychotherapy, others can be attributed to too great a distance between the clitoris and the opening of the vagina. Having come up with this anatomical theory, Marie Bonaparte was delighted to discover Dr Halban of Vienna, a surgeon who had developed an operation which consisted of moving the clitoris closer to the urethral passage. In the 1924 article, signed A. E. Narjani, Marie Bonaparte wrote that five women had been operated on, with positive results. Later, she was forced to admit that the operation was not always one hundred per cent successful.

In December of 1924, after a long illness (salpingitis, or inflammation of the Fallopian tubes), which struck immediately after her father's funeral, and an operation to remove an ovarian cyst, which kept her in bed for three months, Marie Bonaparte (who had virtually unlimited wealth, inherited from her mother's family, the Blancs, who owned the casino at Monte Carlo) imported the plastic surgeon Sir Harold Delf Gillies from London, whom she had met through King George V the previous summer. Gillies performed two operations: first, to 'correct' her breasts, and then, to retouch a scar at the base of her nose, a scar she'd had surgically adjusted twice before. At this time, Marie Bonaparte was forty-two years old and sexually very active, having had a series of passionate love affairs since her marriage to Prince George of Greece and Denmark, who was a closet homosexual, in love with his uncle, Prince Waldemar.

On February 21, 1925, Marie Bonaparte invited Drs René Laforgue and Otto Rank to dinner, to discuss psychoanalysis. She received them in bed, still recuperating from her operations. In April, at Marie Bonaparte's request, Laforgue wrote to Freud, inquiring if he would accept her as a patient for psychoanalysis. In May, she was taking a cure in the south of France for persistent pains in the lower abdomen, pains she and Laforgue believed to have a psychological origin. (These pains seem to have been associated with her chronic pelvic inflammatory disease.) In June, Marie Bonaparte wrote directly to Freud for the first time. In September 1925, in Vienna, she began her analysis with Freud.

They got on like a house on fire. Freud quickly acceded to her request for two hours of his time daily. He enjoyed the '*Prinzessin*', and maliciously confided: 'Lou Andreas-Salomé is a mirror — she has neither your virility, nor your sincerity, nor your style.'[19] It was not long before Marie Bonaparte decided to become a psychoanalyst, and gradually she became close friends with Ruth Mack Brunswick (who later became a junky) and Anna Freud. Marie Bonaparte showed Freud her breast, and discussed his personal finances with him. She gave him a chow, and thereafter the aged Freud became a fervent dog lover. The dogs functioned as a kind of extended family across Europe: puppies were exchanged, dogs were mated, and their deaths lamented. In 1936, Freud wrote to Marie Bonaparte of the 'affection without ambivalence . . . that feeling of an intimate affinity, of an undisputed solidarity', which he felt for his chow, Jo-fi.[20] And in 1938, together with Anna Freud, he translated Marie Bonaparte's book, *Topsy, Chow-Chow au Poil d'Or* — 'Topsy, the Chow with the Golden Hair'.[21]

In July 1926, in Vienna, (after six months of analysis with Freud), Marie Bonaparte had her first consultation with Dr Halban. In the spring of 1927, she had Halban sever her clitoris from its position and move it closer to the opening of her vagina. She always referred to this operation by the name 'Narjani'. The origins of this pseudonym are obscure. The operation, performed under local anaesthesia and in the presence of Ruth Mack Brunswick, took 22 minutes. Freud disapproved. It was 'the end of the honeymoon with analysis'.[22] In May Marie Bonaparte wrote to Freud that she was in despair over her stupidity. Freud, stern but forgiving, it seems, encouraged her to look after her seventeen-year-old daughter, Eugenie, who had been diagnosed as suffering from tuberculosis. Marie Bonaparte felt Freud was reproaching her for her narcissism. In June 1927, the very first issue of the *Revue Française de Psychanalyse*, financed by Marie Bonaparte, came out, and in 1928 she began to practise as an analyst, with Freud himself giving postal supervision.

Marie Bonaparte's conduct of psychoanalysis was from the beginning almost as unorthodox as that of her great enemy, Jacques-Marie Lacan. She would send her chauffeur in a limousine to pick up her patients, to drive them to her palatial home in Saint-Cloud for their sessions. In fine weather, the hour was spent in the garden, with Marie Bonaparte stretched out on a chaise-longue behind the couch. She always crocheted as she listened, indoors or out. In later years, whenever possible, she would take her patients with her, as guests, to her houses in St Tropez or Athens, thus inventing the psychoanalytic house party.

In April 1930, Marie Bonaparte visited Vienna, in order to consult Dr Halban again. The sensitivity in the original place from which the clitoris had been moved persisted. (During this period, Marie Bonaparte was involved in a long affair with Rudolph Loewenstein, was later to become Lacan's analyst, and also analysed her son, Peter.) Halban proposed further surgery on the clitoris, in combination with a total hysterectomy to finally eliminate her chronic salpingitis. Ruth Mack Brunswick was again present at the operation, which took place in May.

In February 1931, Marie Bonaparte had her clitoris operated on by Halban for the third and last time. Throughout this time, of course, Freud was suffering from cancer of the jaw, and undergoing regular operations. Her daughter's health was also very bad during this period, and Eugenie had to have an extremely painful operation on a tubercular cyst in her leg in May 1931.

From very early childhood, Marie Bonaparte was fascinated by murder. Servants' gossip vividly presented the probability that the impecunious and unfeeling Prince Roland, conspiring with his scheming mother, Princess Pierre, had, so to speak, hastened the end of the young heiress, Marie's mother. Marie Bonaparte's very first contribution to the nascent *Revue Française de Psychanalyse* was an essay on 'Le Cas de Madame Lefèbvre',[23] an upper-middle-class woman from the north of France, who had shot her pregnant daughter-in-law in cold blood, while out for a drive with the young couple. Marie Bonaparte's second psychoanalytic essay, published the same year, is entitled: 'Du Symbolisme des Trophées de Tête', or 'On the Symbolism of Heads as Trophies'. The essay investigates the question why the cuckolded husband traditionally wears horns, when otherwise horns are a symbol of virility and power, in both animals and gods. She argues that the relation between castration and decapitation is always played out in terms of the Oedipal drama, and the ridiculous figure of the betrayed husband reconstructs this drama in fantasy, where the laughing spectator unconsciously identifies with the lover, the unfaithful wife stands in for the mother, and the cuckold represents the father. His totemic horns ironically invoke his paternal potency, while the childish wish to castrate (or murder) the father, to turn this threat against him, is sublimated in laughter and derision.[24]

Marie Bonaparte is perhaps most admired for her efficient arrangement of Freud's departure from Vienna in June 1938, after the German invasion of Austria in March of that year. She enlisted the help of the Greek diplomatic corps, and the King of Greece himself, in smuggling Freud's gold out of Austria.[25] On the 5th of June, Freud and his family spent twelve hours in Paris, at Marie Bonaparte's house at rue Adolphe Yvon, sitting in the garden and resting on the long journey from Vienna to London. Freud had not set foot in his beloved Paris since 1889, the summer of the Universal Exposition celebrating the centenary of the Revolution. Marie Bonaparte was also personally responsible for saving Freud's letters to Fliess, a correspondence which Freud himself would have preferred to suppress.[26]

In *Female Sexuality* (1951), Marie Bonaparte wrote at length about the practice of clitoridectomy in Africa, and about the operation that she here called 'the Halban-Narjani operation',[27] in the last section of her book, 'Notes on Excision'. In this text, she once again presents her theories on frigidity in women. Total frigidity, she suggests, where both vagina and clitoris remain anaesthetic, is 'moral and psychogenic, and psychical causes [including psychoanalysis] may equally remove it'.[28] For this reason, she writes: 'The prognosis for total frigidity in women is generally favourable.'[29] Not so the cases of partial frigidity, in which the woman experiences clitoral pleasure, but no vaginal orgasm. Marie Bonaparte considers whether the cultural prohibition on infantile masturbation works in the same way as the practice of clitoridectomy, as an attempt to 'vaginalize' the woman, to internalize the erotogenic zone, and intensify vaginal sensitivity. She concludes that neither method succeeds in 'feminizing' or 'vaginalizing' the young girl, and sees such physical or psychical 'intimidation' as cruel and unproductive.[30]

Earlier in *Female Sexuality*, Marie Bonaparte writes specifically about Halban's operation, referring once again to five cases. Two of these cases could not be followed up, two showed 'generally favourable, though not decisive results',[31] and one was unsuccessful. It is difficult to identify Marie Bonaparte herself among these five cases, although one cannot help suspecting the last. In this case, after the operation, the woman 'had only been satisfied twice in normal coitus, and then only while the cut, which became infected, remained unhealed, thus temporarily mobilizing the essential feminine masochism. Once the cut healed, she had to revert to the sole form of coitus

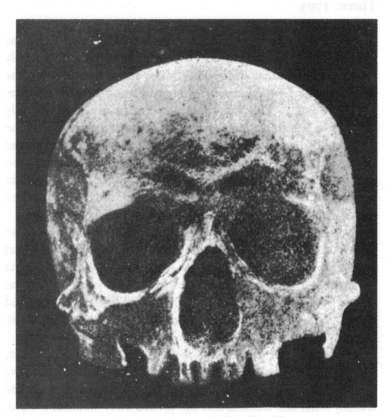

Skull of Charlotte Corday (Fig. 3)

afternoon, she wrote a second letter, again appealing to be allowed a short interview. She ended this letter with the words, '*Il suffit que je sois bien Malheureuse pour avoir Droit à votre bienveillance.*' – 'My great unhappiness gives me the right to your kindness.'[34] She posted this second letter, but Marat was dead before it was delivered.

Corday returned to the rue des Cordeliers at about seven in the evening, hoping to arrive shortly after her second letter. She had spent the afternoon having her hair done; she sent for a hairdresser to come to the hotel, he curled and set her hair, and powdered it lightly. She also changed her outfit. Thinking of Judith of Bethulia, she surmised that Marat was more likely to grant her an audience if she was seductively dressed. She wore a loose spotted muslin dress with a fichu of delicate pink gauze. She tied green ribbons around her high black hat, and once again took a cab to Marat's house.

At the door, Corday argued, first with the concierge and then with Simonne Evrard, until Marat, in his bath, called out to his companion, who went in to him. He would see Charlotte Corday.

Marat was in a tiny room, between the passage and his bedchamber, that was lit by two windows onto the street. He was sitting in a shoe bath, naked, with an old dressing gown thrown across his shoulders. A slab of wood rested across the bath, to serve as a desk, and on this were placed paper, pen, and a bottle of ink tilted by a small bit of wood. His head was wrapped in a cloth soaked in vinegar.

He was near death, as a result of his illnesses, which were various; he suffered acutely from eczema, migraines, herpes, diabetes, arthritis, and neurasthenia. His gastric troubles required him to consume only liquids, and in order to sustain his furious writing practice, Marat drank a minimum of twenty cups of coffee a day. The sores and lesions that covered his body were a horrifying sight; people were often reluctant to sit next to him in the Convention. One expert described his disease as '*l'affection squammeuse et vésiconte*',[35] a sort of generalized scaly eczema. His body deteriorated quickly after his death, although this was partly due to the extreme July heat.

Admitted to his closet, Charlotte Corday talked to Marat briefly about the Girondists at Caen, her fan in one hand and her knife in the other, and then stabbed him, plunging the knife straight downwards into his naked breast. Marat cried out, '*À moi, chère amie, à moi!*'[36] Charlotte Corday was shocked to see Simonne Evrard's distress. There was a tremendous amount of blood, and he died almost immediately. Simonne Evrard and the cook dragged Marat's body out of his bath and tried to put him into bed. Charlotte Corday ventured into the corridor, but the street porter drove her into the salon, where he hit her over the head with a chair. A dentist appeared, followed by a doctor and the commissioner of police for the '*section du Théâtre Français*'. At eight o'clock Corday's second letter arrived; Guellard the police commissioner carefully wrote on it: 'This letter was not delivered . . . it was rendered useless by the admission of the assassin at half-past seven, at which hour she committed her crime.'[37]

David's extraordinary painting, *Marat Assassiné*,[38] shows the Friend of the People dead in his bath, holding in his left hand the letter dated 13 July 1793, with the words clearly legible: '*Il suffit que je sois bien Malheureuse pour avoir Droit à votre bienveillance.*' On the packing case next to the bath lies an *assignat*, or promissory note, with a covering letter from Marat, evidence of his generosity: 'Give this *assignat* to your mother.' The blood-stained knife lies on the floor; Marat's limp right arm hangs down, still grasping his quill pen. On the packing case itself, in Roman capitals, the text: '*À MARAT. DAVID. L'AN DEUX.*' These various texts, in simultaneous juxtaposition within the painting, tell the whole story, David's version of the story. Marat's skin is flawless and very pale.[39]

Historians argue over Charlotte Corday's beauty, the colour of her hair, and even what she was wearing when she committed the murder. After carefully weighing the different accounts, it seems she brought three outfits to Paris with her: the brown dress (before the murder), the spotted muslin (during), and a white dress (after), this last the dress she wore to her trial. To these outfits must be added the red chemise, which she wore to the guillotine, traditional execution dress for murderers, arsonists, and poisoners. On the subject of her hair, it seems to have been 'chestnut', and the tradition that holds her to have been '*blonde cendrée*,' or ash-blonde, was misled simply by the light powder that the hairdresser, M. Person, applied the afternoon of the murder. As for her beauty, it is generally agreed that her chin was very large, a classic sign of degeneracy in Lombroso's theory, though by 1889 the skull was missing its lower jaw, so he never knew this. The only objective account of Charlotte Corday's physical appearance comes from the *laissez passer*, issued at Caen for her trip to Paris. She is described as: 'twenty-four years old, height five feet one inch (*cinq pieds un pouce*), hair and brow chestnut (*châtains*), eyes grey, forehead high, nose long, mouth medium, chin round, cleft (*fourchu*), face oval'.[40] Her height is another area of uncertainty; often described as tall and striking, perhaps '*un pouce*' means two to three inches. Or possibly her traditional Normande hat, with its tall conical crown, added to her stature.

Immediately after the murder, the revolutionary press depicted Corday as a monster: '*une femme brune, noire, grosse et froide*' – '*malpropre, sans grâce . . . la figure dure insolente, érysipèlateuse et sanguine*'.[41] To the Gironde, needless to say, she was indescribably beautiful, an angel. Ironically, Corday's murder of Marat was a bloody turning point in the Revolution; it was arguably the event that precipitated the Terror. In 1836 Marat's sister, Albertine, declared: 'Had my brother lived, they would never have killed Danton, or Camille Desmoulins.'[42] Michelet notes his belief that Marat would have 'saved' Danton, 'and then saved Robespierre too; from which it follows that there would have been no Thermidor, no sudden, murderous reaction'.[43]

On the 16th of July, the funeral of Marat took place. In charge of the design, David passionately wanted to display the

fichu was torn off her neck, and in a moment, it seemed, her head rolled on the ground. Immediately one of Sanson's assistants, a follower of Marat called Legros, ran his knife up the severed neck and held the head high to show it to the crowd, whereupon he gave it a slap, or possibly two or three slaps. The face was seen to blush – not only the cheek that was slapped, but both cheeks, exactly as if she were still able to feel emotion. The spectators were appalled; Michelet writes: 'a tremor of horror ran through the murmuring crowd'.[49]

Much discussion ensued on the likelihood of sensation remaining after decapitation. Scientists entered into elaborate disputations on the *force vitale*, and on whether the head blushed from shame, grief, or indignation. Sanson wrote a letter to the newspaper, condemning the action; he considered it one of the most shameful moments of his career. Legros himself was thrown into jail.[50]

Immediately after the execution, an autopsy was carried out on the body, principally to determine Charlotte Corday's virginity. At the trial she'd been asked how many children she had, and the revolutionary press claimed she was four months pregnant. Perhaps the heroic and virginal figure of Jeanne d'Arc was behind this compulsion to prove Corday promiscuous. In any case, David himself, as a member of the National Convention, attended the autopsy, believing or hoping that 'traces of libertinage' would be found.[51] To his chagrin, her virginity was confirmed. There exists a vivid description of a drawing of this scene:

The body lies outstretched on a board, supported by two trestles. The head is placed near the trunk; the arms hang down to the ground; the cadaver is still dressed in a white robe, the upper part of which is bloody. One person, holding a torch in one hand and an instrument (some kind of speculum?) in the other, seems to be stripping Charlotte of her clothing. Four others are bending forward, examining the body attentively. At the head we find two individuals, one of whom wears the tricolour belt; the other extends his hands as if to say: 'Here is the body, look.'[52]

Historians generally agree that Charlotte Corday's body was buried in Ditch No. 5 in the cemetery at the Madeleine, rue d'Anjou-Saint-Honoré, between Ditch No. 4, which held the corpse of Louis XVI, and No. 6, which would soon receive the bodies of Phillipe Egalité and Marie Antoinette. Chateaubriand was responsible for exhuming the royal remains in 1815, and left a vivid account, in his *Mémoires d'outre-tombe*, of how he recognised the skull of Marie Antoinette, from his recollection of the smile she gave him on one occasion at Versailles in early July 1789, just before the fall of the Bastille:

> When she smiled, Marie Antoinette drew the shape of her mouth so well that the memory of that smile (frightful thought!) made it possible for me to recognise the jaw-bone of this daughter of kings, when the head of the unfortunate was uncovered in the exhumations of 1815.[53]

It remains a mystery, however, precisely how the skull of Charlotte Corday came to be in the collection of Prince Roland Bonaparte. Dr Cabanès, celebrated collector of historical gossip and author of such valuable works as *Le Cabinet Secret de l'Histoire* (1905), *Les Indiscretions de l'Histoire* (1903), and *Les Morts mystèrieuses de l'Histoire* (1901), carried out extensive and thorough research on the provenance of this skull. He learned from Prince Roland that he had acquired it from M. George Duruy, 'who said he would not be sorry to get rid of this anatomical item because it terrified Mme Duruy.'[54] Duruy himself told Cabanès he'd discovered the skull at his aunt's, Mme Rousselin de Saint-Albin; a wardrobe door was standing slightly open, and Duruy spotted the skull sitting on a shelf inside. Mme de Saint-Albin told him it had belonged to her late husband, who was himself convinced it was the skull of Charlotte Corday. Indeed, Rousselin de Saint-Albin had gone so far as to write 'a sort of philosophical dialogue' between himself and the skull, in which they discuss her motives for the crime.[55] Saint-Albin claimed to have bought the skull from an antiquary on the

Quai des Grands-Augustins, who had himself bought it in a sale. Cabanès speculates on the likelihood of the sale in question being that of the *'célèbre amateur'*, Denon, which took place in 1826, but notes that the catalogue of this sale does not mention a skull.[56]

Duruy himself believed that Saint-Albin was in a position to take possession of the skull immediately after the execution, since Saint-Albin was Danton's secretary, and therefore could have obtained the necessary authorization. Cabanès returns to the evidence of the anthropologists who examined the skull at the Universal Exposition of 1889, Bénédikt, Lombroso, and Topinard, who agreed that the skull 'had been neither buried in the earth, nor exposed to the air'.[57] Was the skull dug up immediately, or was it perhaps sold by the executioner, Sanson? Cabanès suggests that the story that is always denied most vehemently is likely to be the true account: that after the autopsy, *'la tête aurait été préparée par quelque médecin et conservée comme pièce curieuse'* – 'the head was *treated* by some doctor and preserved as a curiosity'.[58]

Finally, Cabanès includes, as an appendix to his investigation, a long letter from M. Lenotre, 'the very knowledgable historian of *'Paris révolutionnaire'*,[59] to his friend G. Montorgueil, which was written in the full awareness that the letter would be passed on to Dr Cabanès. In this letter, Lenotre ventures his opinion that the skull is authentic. He argues that there was a thriving trade in body parts and hair of the victims of the guillotine, and points to the later wealth of the Sanson family as evidence that Sanson was 'in a good position to render certain services, to make deals, to traffic a little in the guillotine'.[60] Lenotre goes on to recount an anecdote of the period:

> If (Sanson) didn't sell heads, who did? For there's no question they were sold! One evening in 1793, a woman fainted in the rue Saint-Florentin; she fell; a package she was carrying in her apron rolled into the gutter: it was a head, freshly decapitated . . . She was on her way from the cemetery at the Madeleine,

where a grave-digger had supplied her with this horrible debris.[61]

Lenotre's most striking contribution to the discussion, however, is a description of a dinner party *chez* Rousselin de Saint-Albin:

> One evening, during the reign of Louis Philippe, Saint-Albin invited to dinner a group of friends who were curious about the history of the Revolution. He promised them a sensational surprise. At dessert, a large glass jar was brought in, and removed from its linen case. This was the surprise, and how sensational it was, you can judge, for the glass jar contained the head of Charlotte Corday. Not the skull merely, you understand, but the head, conserved in alcohol, with her half-closed eyes, her flesh, her hair . . . The head had been in this condition since 1793; lately Saint-Albin had decided to have it *prepared* – excuse these macabre details – and wanted, before this operation, to allow his friends the spectacle of this thrilling relic.[62]

Once a head, preserved in alcohol; then a skull, to hold in one's hands, to measure. Now all that remains of Charlotte Corday, the last vestiges of the 'thrilling relic', are three photographs of the skull itself. And yet, how evocative these photographs seem, how poetic, these emblems of castration, perhaps, *memento mori* of the Revolution, these shadowy traces of secret exhumation.

He (Freud) was indignant about the story of the sale (of the Fliess correspondence to Marie Bonaparte) and characteristically gave his advice in the form of a Jewish anecdote. It was the one about how to cook a peacock. 'You first bury it in the earth for a week and then dig it up again.' 'And then?' 'Then you throw it away!'[63]

Notes

1 Sigmund Freud, 'The Uncanny', *Standard Edition* XVII (1919) p. 244.
2 Cesare Lombroso, *The Female Offender* (with Guglielmo Ferrero, London, 1895), p. 33–4.
3 Ibid., p. xvi.
4 Ibid., p. 150–1.
5 See: Gina Lombroso-Ferrero, *Cesare Lombroso: Storie della Vita e delle Opere* (Bologna, 1914), and Luigi Bulferetti, *Cesare Lombroso* (Turin, 1975).
6 Giorgio Colombo, *La Scienza Infelice: Il museo di antropologia criminale di Cesare Lombroso* (Turin, 1975), p. 45.
7 Ibid., p. 45.
8 Dr Paul Topinard, 'À propos du Crâne de Charlotte Corday', *L' Anthropologie* (1890), vol. I, p. 1.
9 Ibid., p. 1.
10 Ibid., p. 3.
11 Ibid., p. 25.
12 Ibid., p. 3.
13 Dr Paul Topinard, 'Le problème des Nègres aux Etats-Unis et sa solution radicale', *L'Anthropologie* (1890), vol. I, p. 382.
14 For Lorianism, see the poetry of Raymond Landau (aka Alexander Task), in Peter Wollen, 'The Mystery of Landau', *Readings and Writings* (London, 1982).
15 Giorgio Colombo, op. cit., p. 57.
16 See: J. Deniker and L. Laloy, 'Les Races Exotiques à l'Exposition Universelle de 1889', parts 1 and 2, *L'Anthropologie* (1890), vol. I, p. 257–294, p. 513–546, which includes sixteen extraordinary photographs by Prince Roland Bonaparte.
17 Celia Bertin, *Marie Bonaparte: A Life* (New York, 1982), p. 39.
18 A. E. Narjani, 'Considérations sur les causes anatomiques de la frigidité chez la femme', *Bruxelles Médical*, April 27, 1924.
19 Celia Bertin, op. cit., p. 155.
20 Letter from Sigmund Freud to Marie Bonaparte of December 6, 1936, No. 288 in Ernst L. Freud (ed.), *Letters of Sigmund Freud* (New York, 1960). I am indebted to Anne Friedberg for drawing my attention to the dogs.
21 Marie Bonaparte, *Topsy, Chow-Chow au Poil d'Or* (Paris, 1937), Sigmund and Anna Freud's translation published in Amsterdam, 1939.
22 Celia Bertin, op. cit., p. 170.
23 Marie Bonaparte, 'Le Cas de Madame Lefèbvre', *Revue Française de Psychanalyse* (1927), vol. I, p. 149–198.

24 Marie Bonaparte, 'Du Symbolisme des trophées de tête', *Revue Française de Psychanalyse*, (1927), vol. I, p. 677–732.

25 See: Ernest Jones, *The Life and Work of Sigmund Freud* (New York, 1953), vol. III, p. 227.

26 See 'peacock anecdote' below, Ernest Jones, op. cit., vol. I, p. 288.

27 Marie Bonaparte, *Female Sexuality* (London, 1953), p. 202.

28 Ibid., p. 202.

29 Ibid., p. 202.

30 Ibid., p. 204.

31 Ibid., p. 151.

32 Ibid., p. 151.

33 Ibid., p. 151.

34 Joseph Shearing, *The Angel of Assassination* (New York, 1935), p. 201.

35 Dr Cabanès, 'La "Lèpre" de Marat', in *Le Cabinet Secret de l'Histoire* (Paris, 1905), p. 164.

36 Dr Cabanès, 'Le Coup de Charlotte Corday', in *Les Indiscretions de l'Histoire* (Paris, 1905), p. 119.

37 Joseph Shearing, op. cit., p. 213.

38 Jacques-Louis David (1748–1825), *Marat Assassiné* 1793, Brussels, Musées Royaux des Beaux-Arts de Belgique.

39 Jean Starobinski, *1789: The Emblems of Reason* (Rome, 1973, trans. Barbara Bray, Cambridge, Mass., 1988), p. 118–119.

40 Dr Cabanès, 'La Vraie Charlotte Corday — était-elle jolie?', in *Le Cabinet Secret de l'Histoire* (Paris, 1905), p. 181.

41 Joseph Shearing, op. cit., p. 230.

42 Jules Michelet, *History of the French Revolution*, (trans. Keith Botsford, Pennsylvania, 1973), vol. VI, Book 12, 'Anarchic Rule of the Hebertists', p. 169.

43 Ibid., p. 169.

44 Joseph Shearing, op. cit., p. 236–7.

45 Ibid., p. 234.

46 Dr Cabanès, op. cit., 'La Vraie Charlotte Corday — était-elle jolie?', p. 188.

47 Dr Cabanès, 'La Vraie Charlotte Corday — Le Soufflet de Charlotte Corday', *Le Cabinet Secret de l'Histoire* (Paris, 1905), p. 198.

48 Christopher Hibbert, *The Days of the French Revolution* (New York, 1981), p. 309.

49 Jules Michelet, op. cit., Book 12, 'The Death of Charlotte Corday', p. 146.

50 Ibid., p. 146.

51 Dr Cabanès, 'La Vraie Charlotte Corday — L'autopsie de Charlotte Corday', *Le Cabinet Secret de l'Histoire* (Paris, 1905), p. 211.

52 Ibid., p. 209.

53 Francois-René [Vicomte] de Chateaubriand, *Mémoires d'outre-tombe* (Paris, 1964), vol. 2. I am indebted to M. Patrick Bauchau for drawing my attention to this reference.

54 Dr Cabanès, op. cit., p. 218.
55 Ibid., p. 219.
56 Ibid., p. 218.
57 Ibid., p. 220.
58 Ibid., p. 221.
59 Ibid., p. 222.
60 Ibid., p. 223.
61 Ibid., p. 224. For traffic in skulls, see also: Folke Henschen, *The Human Skull, A Cultural History* (trans. S. Thomas, London, 1966).
62 Dr Cabanès, op. cit., p. 222–3.
63 Ernest Jones, op. cit., vol. I, p. 288.

Envy

Prelude

It was heaven. The skies were very clear and high, with light clouds scudding across them in high wind, wind that took the form of easy breezes down below. The garden was perfectly landscaped, an ideal balance of cultivation and nature, with wayward paths chancing upon carefully composed views, and the soothing sound of running water, the endless twisting brooks and gentle fountains combining with the distant birdsong to make a natural muzak. The sun fell between the shadowy leaves as we walked, our feet barely touching the damp path, as we floated through paradise, discussing the pros and cons of existence.

I remember Corinne still retained traces of the vehemence, the emotional vehemence that is characteristic of the sublunary sphere. This had the real charm of novelty, for me especially, since I'd avoided the place for so long. It was fading fast, however, gleaming out like sun reflected off a shadowy mirror, a mirror already draped with heavy cloth of gold. Corinne still gleamed, and I walked with her to catch those gleams, and argue through again the oldest conversation, to be or not to be.

Of course she, Corinne, desperately wanted another go. This had all the naïve charm of a puppy or a kitten chasing a ping-pong ball. After a few runs through the mill, most of us are extremely satisfied by things here: reading, walking, enjoying all the things that the specific vehemence of emotion precludes down there. As she spoke, it came back to me, how one could be walking through sublunary gardens, as beautiful as this one (though not so extensive and infinitely varied, of course), and one would be concentrating on a broken heart, some loss or another, tied to a cramp, an ache, an obsession, and the loveliness of the garden would come through in snatches, glimpses, but mostly it merely performed the function of a backdrop to an emotional drama.

What we give up, when we choose to stay here, is desire. And it's not a struggle, we've been through the struggle by then, and we're out the other side. We're quite happy to stumble on melons eternally.

But Corinne, the puppy, wasn't. She wanted to go back. I found it delightful.

'But it's such a lottery, my dear, *who* you get. I mean, you can't *choose*. Not like in the movies, remember that marvellous Hollywood thing with the little girl who *chose* her parents?'

'Yes, they tried to talk her out of it, as well — they said the couple wasn't worth gracing with her presence.'

'Well that's not what I'm saying, sweetheart. I'm just trying to make out why it is that you want to leave . . .'

'Because I *like* it, I like the vehemence that you've let go, sliding out of it like an overcoat slipping off. I want to wear the overcoat, and walk down noisy streets. I want to take my chances. I want to fall in love.'

'It all begins with being a baby, being one thing to one woman, and that love then is where you fall. You never get over that one, you know. Everything later is just a pale shadow of that first substance, an attempt to compensate for that first, inevitable loss —'

'But that's what's so fascinating — I mean, I know you don't know anything about it at the time . . .'

A bird of paradise in all its bright plumage flew past, and we paused, to take a breath and watch.

'But I like the process of attachment, I like the way presence and absence make everything up for the baby: language, skin, bodies — existence *is* that oscillation of attachment and separation.'

'Not everyone would agree with you there . . .'

'It feels like an ocean, I want to swim in it.'

'There are some very nice beaches here, you know.'

'I know.'

'It's the suffering, and the endless *changing*, and the terrible *confusion* that I'm so happy without. I like this clarity, but then I suppose I had my fill of confusion.'

'I *have* chosen my parents anyway.'

'*What?*'

'Well I'm working on it.'

'You must be joking, that's a fundamental rule of existence — it's arbitrary.'

'Well, not completely. Not completely arbitrary. I mean, there's all the genetic stuff . . .'

'But that's just the existential necessities, hard facts like weather or geography.'

'*Angels* are allowed to make specific interventions.'

'That's not your sphere. You're *not* an angel. You're just — what do they call it — you're just a ghost.'

'Don't be horrible to me.'

'I'm sorry, Corinne. But this really is unheard of.'

'I'm setting a precedent. I'm working on it.'

'And they're taking this seriously?'

'I've been listening in. And I've been *dreaming* —'

'I had no idea.'

'— and I know where I want to go.'

'I should have guessed. I should have distracted you. I thought your attraction to that place was *sweet*. Now I realize it's more like an obsession.'

'But I'm persuading them. It's specific, and justified, and also something of an experiment.'

'OK, tell me about it . . .'

'In this dream, I was a woman . . .'

Chlamydia

Everyone was reproducing, suddenly. The magazines named '*a baby*' as the fashionable accessory of 1988. Jeanie realized she'd been avoiding friends with babies, doubled over inside with the intensity of her feeling. She was like a miser who cannot bear to visit someone who ostentatiously displays their wealth. The extremity of her desire for a child was a dark, heart-clenching secret, and though she joked about it, no one knew how completely it had come to shape her days. By making jokes, she deflected attention, even her own attention, from the agonizing exigencies of her wish.

And, she thought, maybe it's true, that wanting is just an endless series, that once you get *a*, you long for *b*, and once *b* dissolves in the mists of time, *c* looms over the horizon, all holding out that same crazed promise: some kind of relation, contact, collision with some other, something *else*.

Jeanie found herself imagining the body of a child, as she walked down the street, on everyday expeditions, to the supermarket, the dry cleaner. The soft skin, round arms, kicking legs of a baby came to mind, in the ordinary reverie of everyday. In bed, lying against Stephen, she pictured herself, sculptured herself into an eight-year-old, fitting so easily into the shape made by his sleepy body. In imagination, she became smaller, and Stephen like a great green hill, or large animal, that, child-ish, she could curl up against. She imagined lifting up a two-year-old, a three-year-old, standing holding the child on her right hip, supporting it with her arm, easily, easily, and laughing easily with another woman, standing, holding a kid on her hip. (She never imagined breastfeeding a baby, as if that would be going too far, indulging herself too much.) She could place herself in the kitchen, in imagination, and have a kid walk in, from school maybe. She could hold a baby in her two hands, against her shoulder, the baby's face next to her neck.

There were more and more women friends with babies now, more and more people to avoid. It was just as she'd always predicted, as they hit thirty-three, thirty-four, thirty-five, they reproduced. She couldn't bear to see them. She avoided them. She dreamed constantly of having a baby and something going terribly wrong.

With their children on their laps, young mothers would advise against it. Wait a little longer, they said, it's really hard work. They'd insist how impossible her present way of life would become: no more restaurants, travelling, no more going out. She met friends whose twelve-week-old baby had never slept more than a couple of hours at a time. They looked haggard, traumatized. They looked like they were having a nervous breakdown. Jeanie listened as Simon spoke of the intransigence of his tiny son, his sense of horror at the intensity of the baby's demand, the baby's body twisting, straining furiously in his arms, screaming blue murder. The young man with his exhausted eyes told her his baby son was a monster.

Jeanie thought of a baby as something that would give her exactly what she had to have, precisely meet her needs. Her wish had all the urgency and thrill of unrequited love. And she went through all the usual things, the familiar routines of mistaken love: enraged frustration (*why* can't I have it?), unreal expectation (. . . and we would love each other for ever and ever, endlessly . . .), fantasies of physical intimacy so vivid as to be hallucinatory (. . . the back of your neck, pale eyes looking, wet mouth . . .).

Freud is quite explicit: the only thing that can possibly *really* give satisfaction to a woman, castrata, is the baby she produces, the baby that represents the phallus, represents her desire. In theory. In practice a baby keeps you up all night until you can't think, or work. Jeanie read in the paper, the women's page, how reading a book uninterrupted becomes a forgotten luxury. This meant everything and nothing to her, wanting as she did the total transformation of herself that she imagined giving birth would bring, and believing at the same time that the specific pleasures of solitude were something she couldn't do without.

Jeanie pictured her mother surrounded by kids, on a beach, with Jeanie herself as a child, Jeanie's sisters. Her mother was so pretty, with her 'great legs', in shorts, sitting on the sandy beach, the sun pale yellow everywhere, and the kids, five-year-olds, three-year-olds, playing in the sand, with the small long waves coming in. Like a snapshot, it was the fifties beach scene. Her mother calling out, to put some more Nosecote on her nose. Standing still, the tedium of sun lotion. Rubbing sun block onto naked shoulders and back of the five-year-old girl, a floppy white sunhat and red bathing suit, cotton with small white flowers, a plastic spade in her fist. Her mother was younger, then, than Jeanie now — in this scene, where kids wandered off and came back, her mother talking so easily, laughing as she sits on the beach towel, her legs making triangles before her, sunglasses on, laughing with another woman lying beside her.

What was so terrible about these daydreams, what upset Jeanie so much, was the way they came unbidden, uncalled for. It was as if her desire came to her, welling up from inside; she had not given herself permission to want this. Something between a memory and a fantasy, her wish was painful, bringing tears as it rose up from the depths. She could play all the parts in these scenes: the child standing still, reluctantly (stand still, just for a minute, while I put this on), looking out across the sand to the small waves, and then the mother, rubbing sun lotion over the child's back, her little shoulder blades and sweet neck in the shadow of the white cotton hat. Jeanie could be in both these bodies, and be the camera, circling around them, taking in the surroundings, the constant swish of waves breaking, the sense of wet sand giving under bare feet. She could pan across the beach, close-up on the child's neck (mother's p.o.v.), stare out towards the other kids digging in the wet sand (kid's p.o.v.), Jeanie could make the whole thing up, against her will.

Sometimes it seemed that envy divided the world up for her, into men and women. Men she despised, and pursued. Women she adored, they had a reality that men lacked, it was women who counted, so to speak, yet everything she did was a repudiation of the pleasures of femininity. She excluded herself from the secret life of the harem, that easy, laughing world of women and children. This is not for you, she felt. Jeanie built high walls, and planted trees and lawns, made a sunny beach, to put her imaginary women in — a grove of trees with oranges and lemons, flowers, birds — she put them there, like playing with dolls, she placed them in the garden, laughing easily, and built high walls, and locked herself out. It didn't matter that she knew this heavenly garden existed only in her imagination. This was the place she couldn't go, and as such it was very important to her.

So she used these images to draw boundaries, clean lines through the world: men wore suits, made money, pursuing empty goals, unable to make connections. Women wove webs of relation, an arm around a sleepy child. She placed herself outside both these realms, over here, where we undo family ties, mistrust longing, repudiate dependency, and stand alone. Over here, with the other oddballs. We cook when we please, and sleep badly. We fall in love relentlessly. We know the inside of the clinics well, the different illnesses we are particularly prone to: the infections, viruses, and unwanted pregnancies of this solitary life. Romance, romance: the shine on the nose, that gleam of glamour putting an edge on everything. I can picture myself with a hard edge, in my black overcoat, white face, red lipstick, in the cold city street. Where does this picture come from? Fashion photographs? A set of fictions: on my right, the harem garden I name paradise, forever excluding me; on my left, the businessmen in their dark-grey suits, and here, before me, the woman imagining herself being seen, the hard edge of a black coat against the noisy city.

These were the cards she'd dealt herself, glossy and flat, a set of impenetrable fictions with almost no connection to anything else or anyone — Jeanie played out her cards, occasionally jostled by another, like someone accidentally bumping into you in the street, an unexpected touch you can neither anticipate nor control. Occasionally jostled by some fragment of real life, she continued to pore over her cards, turning them in sequence, like a tarot reader for whom the images have taken on all the intensity of real life.

Tuesday: *On the phone. Bette and Jeanie talked on the phone a lot.*

J : I think about it all the time, *dream* about babies —

B : Really?

J : All the time. It's an obsession. Endlessly thinking about what you can't have or don't have, or might have —

B : It's like a fantasy boyfriend, you can imagine everything being so great —

J : Yes, it's a boyfriend-in-fantasy when you're twenty-five, and a baby-in-fantasy when you're thirty-five — what you haven't got. And then I guess it's also about the future, right, a metaphor of our love for each other extending indefinitely, our *attachment*.

B : Since you won't get married.

J : Yes, it's the only way to *say*, let's stick together for the unforeseeable future. Saying let's have a baby is just a way to say I do love you, really I do.

B : So actually having a baby would be a mistake.

J : I don't know. In this dream I had a baby and I didn't know if it was a boy or a girl, it had no name. It's as if I'd *forgotten*. This was *terrible*.

B : Mmm.

J : And there was another dream in which I had a baby and I put it in the airing cupboard, to keep warm, but I forgot about it, I went out, and while I was out I suddenly remembered the baby and I was sure it was dead by now.

B : Wow. You have *lots* of these dreams?

J : Yup.

B : But they're all about neglecting the baby, forgetting about it. Maybe it's not a baby at all, maybe it's (what they call) *part* of you . . .

J : Oh yeah — my analyst always used to say, *part* of you, and I'd think, my left ear . . .

B : So what's suffocating in the airing cupboard? Your work?

J : Obviously my work. It goes without saying my work. It's all this flight from femininity lark, this — can't be a man, won't be a woman routine.

B : Are there other dreams?

J : I always forget the best ones.

Monday: *On the phone.*

J : I think I've got this problem with my sister, you know, she's got the babies, I get the books. Like you *can't* have both.

B : It's like Connie and Isabel, division of labour, they couldn't both wear jeans, even.

J : When I have long hair, Louise has short hair, and vice versa. Always.

B : When Isabel sold her car, Connie finally learned to drive.

J : Are we so envious, so scared of taking things away from each other?

B : It's being scared of being too alike, it's identifying so much that you have to go to incredible lengths to distinguish yourself, to make sure you're not one and the same.

J : But are we scared of obliterating or being obliterated! It's like feeling, it could've been *me*. You look at — I look at my sister, and I feel, that's me, *but.*

B : So what's stopping you?

J : I don't know, I mean, I'm the girl who has abortions, right, not the one with the sweet little offspring in the pram.

B : Humph.

J : And then there's all the illness stuff, I probably can't have kids anyway, because of my blocked tubes, chlamydia, the clap, and then if I do manage to conceive, I'm a million times more likely to miscarry than most people, because of all my illnesses, my weird cervix, etc. That's if it's not an ectopic pregnancy which I'm even *more* prone to . . . Every time I get a symptom, I think, chlamydia. Not that again, not the ugly spectre of infertility, that old ghost, come to haunt me again. Again.

Thursday: *On the phone.*

B : It's so difficult —

J : — being a Woman . . .

B : No — wow, you're there already? I'm still at the transvestite stage —

J : Join the queue!

B : No, really, I used to feel just like a transvestite, I used to wear these trousers, very very tapered *indeed*, and you know, a sweater, and I had these high heels, the heels were worn down a bit, I really liked them but the heels were a little too high for me — and then I had this really lovely handbag of my godmother's, with a little handle, and I'd wear it as a shoulder bag, you know, tucked right *under*, but it would slide down, of course, and I'd end up holding it by the handle, in my hand — and I remember at work one time, I was working in the Merchandise Mart in Chicago, I remember this woman who worked there looked at me one day and said, 'I see, when you were a little girl someone told you that grown-up ladies wear high heels and carry little *hand*bags.' There I was, tottering slightly in these shoes, and clutching this bag — like a child, or a transvestite.

J : That's it — dressing up in mummy's clothes. That's all we can do.

B : Yes, but let's face it, we're fondly imagining that there's some femininity out there somewhere that *isn't* like that, that's real, authentic. The madonna, the woman with the child in her arms. And lots of people kneeling at her feet, preferably.

44

J : It must be awful to have a baby and feel just as strange about it as we feel in our high heels and handbags. I expect it happens all the time.

B : What a ghastly thought.

Monday: *On the phone.*

J : We went to see these people, these old friends of Stephen's, and you know, they live in this fantastic house, and she's really *stunning*, she's got Kirghiz eyes, and he's great, they're both great, and they have this sweet kid, in pyjamas, going to bed, and I just thought, I'll never have that, never never never, I'll never have a house with high ceilings and long windows and a garden with a *tree* in it, and it was like I was just overcome with envy — the sense of loss — like its *too late*.

B : But why is it too late?

J : It's just that you make choices, and all along the way you have to recognize what you're giving up, what's falling by the wayside. It's like you realize what you're precluding by being the person you are.

B : This sounds ridiculous to me.

B : My friend Penelope's analyst always used to say: Envy, use it! You want it, get it! Don't writhe in torment, do it! I always thought this was the most useful thing anybody's analyst had ever said *ever*.

B : So?

J : So I don't *really* want to live that Other Life, I just feel this loss, when I know I can't, when I'm forced to acknowledge that it's not an option.

B : It's like in AA they say, this is not a dress rehearsal.

J : Mmm.

Tuesday: *On the phone.*

J : Can I read you this bit I found about narcissism and having babies?

B : If you must.

J : It kills me, this stuff. He says: *Even for narcissistic women, whose attitude to men remains cool*, check it out, *there is a road to complete object love.* That's what we want, right? Object Love. So, he says: *In the child which they bear, a part of their own body confronts them like an extraneous object, to which, starting out from their narcissism, they can then give complete object love.* I love that bit about the extraneous object, it's like a horror movie.

B : I think it's all nonsense. I mean when it comes to real life.

J : I think it's true.

B : Not in practice, not really.

J : Really.

B : Jesus. No wonder you're so fucked up.

J : Thanks a lot. I had another dream.

B : OK. Fire away.

J : I don't think there's much interpreting to do, it fits right in with your theory about my work . . .

B : Tell me the dream, I've got to go.

J : In the dream I was going to *adopt* a newborn baby, because I wanted one *right away.* But when it appeared, it was a fucked-up little girl (*already* damaged, a girl with a history), instead of the baby *boy* (now it was gender specific, suddenly) that I'd expected. I sent her back, or thought of sending her back.

B : And how is it about your work?

J : Well I think it's about my wish that one day I'll just wake up and suddenly *become* this different person, you know, I imagine this entirely *new* (phallic?) writing will be mine — but of course it can't happen, I'll always only have the confused, confusing —

B : Castrated —

J : — fucked-up little girl. It's what I've *got.*

B : That sounds logical. So once again it's not about babies at all.

46

J : Nope, that's right. Just about me. I thought, if I ever had a daughter, I could name her Chlamydia.

Friday: *On the phone.*
B : I had this dream, in this dream I was a woman, and — I mean, I was *specifically* a woman, which is *most* unusual — anyway, I was this woman, but . . .

Tuesday: *On the phone.*
B : I had this friend who could never imagine herself envied. It was as if she had a block, she couldn't even contemplate it for a second. I figured it was all about insisting that she was the most deprived of all, and for me to suggest that she did have something, anything, that others could envy, was like being very cruel to her, saying something horrible, because she needed so much to be the envier, and never the envied.
J : People like that get really carried away when the wheel turns, though, and they really enjoy being in the position of the envied one. Like all those years of suppressed showing off, of denying you have anything at all – when things change, and they can finally afford to admit it, it's amazing, they're the ones who really dig it. Narcissistic gratification. They positively gloat.
B : I don't know if that's true. I don't think so. I think most of the time they never get there, they remain enviers forever.

Suddenly Jeanie saw herself from outside: enviable. It was like looking over her own shoulder, like when the camera is just behind the protagonist, placing him firmly in the picture. Most of the time she felt detached from the world, which, like a movie, swirled on without her. But suddenly she saw herself, in enviable terms. No kids encumbering, no tiny hands clutching at her knees, no baby vomit on her black sweater.

Independence: her own flat, with windows, and pictures on the wall. The noisy street outside, buses rumble past, to remind her of this busy city: no gentle tree-lined streets for her. No pram-pushing down the tree-lined street, the baby carry-cot on the back seat of the Renault, off to the giant Sainsbury's, stocking up. A freezer. None of that. She went out, with Stephen, almost every night. Occasionally, cheques came in the post, for work she'd done. Books arrived, to review. People telephoned, asking her to appear here, or there. She kept trying different hairdressers. She bought shoes. Sometimes she received unsolicited gifts, in the form of notes from people who admired her work. Somehow, most of the time she forgot about these things. They were invisible to her. She longed for a child.

Jeanie went to visit a friend with kids. It was hell. She saw herself from outside, suddenly: enviable.

My longing for a child percolates through the semi-permeable stone of these dark grey days, poisoning the well. Conversations are riddled with obscure or secret references to this possibility, as if my ears are always pricked, hoping for the signal that will quell my anxiety, make the decision. If only I could give it up, or pursue it; as it is, I'm frozen, my feet set in cement, stuck in this moment of the mourning of possibility.

Tears in the bath, hot, lying in hot water with hot tears on my face, my hand flat on my belly, suddenly remembering feeling so sick this morning, and thinking: *maybe I'm pregnant.* An immediate sensation of terror, then some rapid calculations, ovulation, sex, nine months from now would be? Horror. Then, with no warning, tears, for my longing, to have a baby inside me, is complete and overwhelming.

Note: Melanie Klein's (staggering) contention that little girls don't find the same satisfaction in masturbation that little boys do, because of their sense of internal organs, the 'receptive quality' of the vagina which produces a longing for penetration. Of course, I didn't know I had a vagina, so my receptive quality must be impaired. But there's a difference between a wish to be penetrated (which is all about crossing a boundary, the thin line that holds my body together, the surface of my skin), and a wish to have something inside you (which could be a baby, or a penis, or an ideal image of oneself, even?). Possibly. I used to imagine myself like a small figurine inside the great shell of my body. As if my body were hollow, and there were great dark voids between the surface of my skin and the little person inside me. That's very different to imagining a baby, who is always curled up perfectly or under water. These hot tears, now, salty like the amniotic fluid in the womb.

Tracing ambivalence, how does it go: first, the shocking thought. Nausea. Terror. Calculations: when did I ovulate, when did we fuck, when is my period due, when would the baby be born? Horrified disbelief: it's not possible. Pregnancy test: you can buy kits at the chemist. You can go to your GP. Sudden thought of abnormality: my blocked tubes (ectopic), my diseases (spontaneous abortion), my fucked-up cervix. My inability to give birth. More terror. And then the thought of the little child inside me, possibly, and tears, too many tears, in the hot water. Feeling sick.

A book would perform all the functions of a baby, she thought, writing another book. It would occupy her time and energy, make demands, be messy and shitty and wet and uncontrollable, and it would scream at times, and at times it would sleep (she would sleep), and in the end, just like a baby, it would speak to her, saying things she didn't expect. On the borders of sleep, hypnagogic, she pictured a baby, wrapped in white lacy robes, wearing a little bonnet, and then, like Alice holding the pig, she saw herself holding, like a baby in her arms, a large round log of wood, with sawed ends, coarse bark, in a lacy bonnet and white baby blanket. She knew it represented the raw material of the paper of the book that would take the place of her wish for a baby. It was heavy and solid, as writing isn't, heavy and solid as her wish. She woke up, and decided to *transfer* her desire. Later Bette pointed out that log means a kind of book, a journal. Jeanie felt that sense of flurried excitement, the elation that comes when one inadvertently comes upon the dreamwork.

When I had PID, it was amazing, how painful it was. I remember that I couldn't stop moving. I kept writhing, I had to keep moving, turning, on my bed. At one point Stephen touched me, gently, he put his hand on my side, and I couldn't bear it, I recoiled. Rose was here from New York, and Connie, and Stephen — all these horrified faces, looking down at me, they were pale with horror. And me just writhing in pain.

It was really awful, but there's some comic bits . . . Stephen amazingly had just sprained his ankle. I'd made him jump over a tree in Kew Gardens, he'd jumped over my bed suddenly and I was incredibly impressed, I never knew he could *jump*, and then a few days later, when we were at Kew with the Russians, I said, for a joke, Stephen can jump! And so he did, and sprained his ankle, badly, and was in the most amazing pain. He drank a lot of rum, and smoked dope, and refused to go to hospital. And, like, the *next day*, I suddenly collapsed. I was alone in the house, and Rose was arriving from New York, and I began to be in the most terrible pain.

I went out, to throw myself into the doctor's surgery across the road, but they were closed between twelve and two-thirty, and I was standing in the street in the most terrible pain, it was five past twelve, and I thought I saw one of the doctors from the practice a little way down the street, but I was too embarrassed to accost him, to say, are you a doctor, help me. This is a sign of how my brain wasn't functioning any more. I was completely desperate. I left the keys for Rose at the off-licence across the road, and collapsed into bed. The telephone rang, it was Rebecca Marshall to ask me to lunch, and I was all right for a bit and then I was crying uncontrollably, I couldn't breathe or speak, and she realized I was alone and completely freaking out and said, I'll be right over. So Rose walked in from the airport, full of beans, and then Rebecca appeared, with a flower, and I was (literally) writhing in agony. It seemed impossible to wait two hours until the surgery reopened. I had no idea what to do. Rose said, don't you know any other doctors? This was a revelation. I remembered my mother's private doctor. I telephoned, they said it was OK to come and see his colleague. It was in Wimpole Street though and I had no idea how I was going to get there. I said, I'm not sure I'm going to be able to drive. Rose said: We'll take a taxi. I had completely forgotten that taxis existed.

At that time I had this IUD, I'd had it for about nine months, it was an experimental IUD called the T-Nova, it could be left in for four years, and it had copper *and* silver wrapped around it. I pictured it like an earring embedded in my womb. The FPA had refused to give me an IUD, they said if I ever wanted to have children I shouldn't, not with my history. That the risk of infection was too strong. Then I fell in love with Stephen, and we would do sex all the time, and I was extremely anxious about getting pregnant, mainly the problem of renewing sperm-icide, because even then I couldn't use those pessaries, anyway I was terribly worried about it and I decided to get an IUD so I wouldn't have to worry. I tricked the FPA into giving it to me, I said that I'd already had the appointment they insist on, to discuss the IUD, the pros and cons, I lied, basically, to get them to give me the IUD right away. And they did, and they gave me a new, experimental one, with silver as well as copper, which I pictured as a beneficent earring nestled in my womb. Until I started writhing with pain.

Pelvic inflammatory disease is caused by bacteria getting inside your uterus and travelling up your Fallopian tubes. They think they climb up the nylon string that's attached to the IUD, the string they use to pull it out. Chlamydia is the name of a particularly lethal one of these string-climbing organisms. It's only recently been isolated and named, so it isn't in the books yet, the only people who've heard of it are the women who've had it. Anyway, when you have an orgasm, your uterus makes a spasmodic movement, that can actually suck things into itself, so the IUD is really most suitable for non-orgasmic women who've already had children. Because then infertility isn't such a problem.

The Wimpole Street doctor said, it's either a pelvic infection or it's appendicitis. I'd been unable to sit still in the taxi, continuous writhing, but the pain left me almost completely when I was flat on my back on the examination table in his enormous office. This often happens to me with doctors; I am so frightened of them my symptoms disappear. He gave me a scrip for a double dose of antibiotics. He described how the pain would change if it was appendicitis, and how in that case, I should go to the hospital. He said he didn't believe that IUDs cause pelvic infection and there was no need to take it out, although some doctors did remove it when this happened. I went home and went to bed. It was Friday. I spent the weekend in bed, too ill to eat, even.

I took very painkiller in the house — Italian diarrhoea pills with opium, some leftover Distalgesic. The pain was completely hypnotic, I was unable to think about anything else. Then on Monday morning things were suddenly much worse. Connie called in the doctor from the surgery across the street, an emergency, she said, and he came right away. I was way out there, far beyond any ability to make decisions or even speak. The doctor was furious he hadn't been called sooner. He said he would take the IUD out at three that afternoon. After he left I fell into a state of abject terror; the terror even overcame the pain. I remembered all the times an IUD had been put in

or taken out, I remembered the time I screamed as they pulled out the Copper 7, the first one, at the health clinic at college, in 1975. I couldn't face it. I was in a state of abject terror, I couldn't cry or talk, it was just this terrible gasping, and writhing. And then my body saved me. It was as if I just couldn't take any more, I'd reached the limit. I sank into a heavy sleep, in that white room, I became unconscious. There was no warning: the pain receded, sleep appeared out of nowhere, I knew nothing.

At ten to three, Connie woke me up, time to go to the doctor. I was so sleepy it was like having taken a load of tranquillizers. Instead of the writhing, sobbing, out of control, flailing terror, I had become a heavy, pale body, almost sleep-walking across the street. I asked the doctor for intravenous valium; he said, we'll try to do it without, but I promise if you can't bear it, we'll give you something. This seemed reasonable; I was capable of being reasonable. It was as if I was in slow motion; having been in a panic, high pitched, shrieking, I was sleep-walking, very very calm.

On the table, lying on my back, Connie held my hand and talked to me. The doctor put the speculum in, and couldn't find my cervix. He dug around with it for a while. He was somewhat in awe of our tremendous presence, rather wonder-fully and appropriately humble, so when I calmly said, I suggest you take the speculum out, and stick your finger in to *feel* where the cervix is, and *then* put the speculum back in, he wasn't offended, incredibly, and he did it.

The first time an IUD was put into me, a nurse came in, to literally hold my hand and talk about *anything* else — what I was studying, where I was born, etc. This is incredibly irritating, but very effective as a distraction. It's almost impossible to reply politely to a stranger's questions, and at the same time hold your whole body in fear, anticipating the moment of pain. Unthinking, Connie and I automatically did this. I said, this is so funny, it reminds me of the story of when I was born. Connie said, yes. I said, you know it. And *she* said (brilliantly),

tell Dr Green. So I launched into this primal anecdote, occupying the upper part (so to speak) of my mind, while my body took deep breaths, laid out flat with my legs spread wide, readying itself for this moment of intense pain. I was expecting, or it was expecting this pain to be inconceivable, but there was also some sense that when the IUD was out, it would be the beginning of the end of this, the beginning of the possibility of getting better. At the same time (this was part of the terror before my sleep) I knew Dr Green wasn't an expert; he wasn't a doctor who took out IUDs every day, like at the FPA. In the terror, I'd reasoned with myself, before the sleep came, I'd said, what is the worst that can happen? The worst is that my uterus will be perforated when the IUD is taken out and I will never be able to have children. This is *not* the worst thing in the whole world. It's terrible, but *much* worse things can happen to you. It's as if I made my peace, so to say, with this worst, persuaded myself it wasn't unbearable, and then I could crash out.

On the table, of course, I didn't think of that; I thought of nothing, something else entirely. As the doctor tinkered around in my vagina, I told the story of my mother, how she insisted that the baby was coming, no one believed her, she insisted on going to the hospital, and then she was left alone in a labour room with a student nurse, and eventually, suddenly, this *foot* appeared (my foot), coming out of her vagina, whereupon the nurse exclaimed, Jesus Christ! and ran out of the room. That's the end of the story. After years of hearing it, I finally asked her, so what did you do then? And she said, I took hold of that foot and pulled as hard as I could, I wanted you *out* of there.

And Connie was laughing, and the doctor pulled, and I felt this slight sensation, of something slipping deep inside me, and Dr Green said, it's out, it's all over, and I gasped, I said, I don't believe it, it's out? And the doctor said, it was half out already, it was digging into your cervix, that's why you were in such terrible pain.

I don't remember what happened after that. The relief blew through me like cool air, filling me up, no more pain, no more terror. There was an image of a T-shaped earring with its caul of blood and phlegm, I was so glad to have this thing *out* of me. I hadn't realized how impossible it was for me to imagine getting well, being well, I couldn't *picture* my uterus without this silver and copper object, this T-Nova in there, poisoning me.

I stayed in bed for weeks, I was amazingly ill, and slowly I got better again. I watched *Notorious* on TV. And it was almost funny to remember that mental argument, when I persuaded myself that infertility wasn't the worst thing that can happen to you, because of course what really would have been unthinkable, what would have been impossible to bear, was if the pain I was feeling then were to go on. And in a way, coming up with the idea of a life unable to have children was, like the story of my birth, coming up with a distraction, in the form of a rationalization, in order to get away from the agony of my body, and my terror of more pain to come.

The analyst was bored.

People suffered so much, it was unbelievably wearing to maintain his defences, keep the psychic raincoat on as they poured their unhappy words over him, sitting silently there. (He wouldn't call it a psychic raincoat. That was wrong.)

People suffered so much, more of the same, more of the same. Sometimes his interest would be piqued by a new combination, almost like the pleasant surprise of seeing someone wearing intentionally clashing colours, an emerald green hat angled on shocking pink hair, different colour fluorescent socks. (He doesn't think like that, this is all wrong.)

People suffered so much, it was hard to keep up the façade, hard not to suffer with them. Sometimes that simple process, of maintaining his defences, took up almost all his energy. (He doesn't use words like energy.)

The analyst was bored.

On and on, this endless suffering, and not one of his patients had made a joke for days. It goes without saying that he wasn't allowed to; occasionally he didn't even allow himself to laugh at one of theirs, replying instead with one of the classic formulae, so sententious, about how it really isn't very funny is it, etc. etc. Turning bitter laughter into tears, that was part of his job. And never crying himself, refusing laughter often, to get at the deeper feelings that he knew were there. November and February were the worst months for jokes; he blamed the weather. As Christmas and Easter, with their long breaks, approached, the misery and resentment of the patients, soon to be deprived of the analyst, often generated sequences of black comedy unmatched in any sphere. It was always the most intelligent clients who had to be deflected from these forays into bitter humour. But most of the time, it was familiar territory, mothers and fathers and lovers and how hurt, how damaged and hurt we all are.

What does the analyst envy? I envy the analyst; what does the analyst envy?

To Jeanie the question seemed extraordinarily profound. It was like turning the tables, upsetting the couch. As a rule, they were meant to be concerned only with Jeanie's feelings, her very private agonies and pleasures. Of course, imagining the analyst's envy was only another way of putting Jeanie's unconscious fantasies into words, bringing them to mind. That's what the analyst would have thought. But for Jeanie, alone in her room, it was a revelation to even consider the analyst, the great man, as possibly envious. For her, it felt like a huge leap into objectivity, into a sense of real history. It also seemed like an unanswerable question.

The analyst envies other analysts. The analyst envies younger analysts starting out on their training analysis, when the whole world of psychoanalysis is just opening up and still has its tremendous depth and glamour. The analyst envies those patients who terminate, who are not seduced into the endless project of becoming an analyst themselves. (There are three ways to terminate: the analyst leaves the country, the patient leaves the country, the patient decides to become an analyst. It wasn't a joke.) The analyst envies those patients who leave the country? She stopped. That didn't sound right, especially as she was intending to leave the country. The analyst envies the artist, who has access to the unconscious in ways the analyst cannot understand or control. Speaking as an artist, she felt the analyst ought to envy this. Perhaps he didn't though, perhaps that was part of the problem. She felt that she bought his line on what she ought to envy, the house, the garden, the kids, the family, the career, it was pretty easy to be persuaded that all one's feelings of exclusion and distress were valid, substantial, and that you really should devote yourself to getting some of these things. But maybe he didn't see what she had, something that maybe he ought to want more, to envy.

Monday: *On the couch.*
J : The problem is, babies, yes babies, I want one. Badly.
Dr Q : Yes.
J : But if I want one, if I allow myself to want one — it's a
    problem, because it opens up a whole new can of gynaeco-

logical worms, so to speak.

Dr Q : . . .

 J : I mean, it's difficult to choose to want something that *maybe* I won't be able to have — because of all the predispositions and illnesses and things.

Dr Q : Go on.

 J : You see it would be a bit of a *risk* really, I don't want to go through a series of miscarriages or whatever, and maybe not be able to have one; it's a real risk — of possibly plunging yet further into the nightmare black abyss of illness and doctors and gynaecological trouble, just a reconfirmation of the sense of damage, my sense of femininity as damage, damagedness.

Dr Q : . . .

 J : On the other hand, I think possibly I would be someone who would be very happy if I *did* have a baby, because it would be a *making good* of all this nightmare sense of damage and illness and difficulty that's so established, integral, like tiny roots through my body. I think I would be very *pleased* if out of all this dark abyss of gynaecology and trouble would come this good thing, this baby.

Dr Q : Yes.

 J : So once again all this stuff just comes back to fantasies about *oneself*. I always used to be so vehement about the rights of the child — you know, really angry at the idea of parents reproducing for their own egotistical reasons, and yet here I am, finding this business of thinking of having a baby in order to make good my own bodily history *makes sense*. It's weird.

Dr Q : . . .

 J : I suspect it's my age, you know, when you're fourteen you think it's outrageous that your parents had you without really *meaning* to, that is, for their own foolish reasons. I always figured they were like, on automatic, anyway, the fifties family and its two point four kids. And now I'm approaching the reproductive deadline, of *course* having babies is something you do for your own pleasure — what other reason could there be?

Dr Q : What other reason do you think there could be?

The analyst envies people who don't do jobs like this.

Analysis as a profession was like being a dentist: there were those who advocated flossing, those who did extractions, those who concentrated on straightening teeth and those who were mostly concerned with preventing disease. But basically it was the same, probing into the wet dark rotten inner recesses of someone's head, overcoming inevitable disgust at signs of neg-lect and corruption, the furry tongue, the blackened molar, the broken, jagged edge of a damaged tooth, all this in the higher cause of scientific detachment, medical objectivity, the only sure path to enlightenment. Using the same shiny instruments over and over, those sententious phrases he absolutely relied on, with the same problems emerging again and again. The sexual element was there too. Lying down is always a difficult pleasure, and everyone has sadomasochistic dentist fantasies, everyone knows that sensation of being at his mercy, the frisson of terror that lies within one's necessary submission and depen-dence. And of course dentistry, like psychoanalysis, was funda-mentally all about pain, pain and beauty.

Jeanie found it hard to imagine that anyone would ever want to be a dentist.

Interlude

Corinne sat in the huge room, as pale light flooded through the tall windows, throwing bright oblongs over the long tables.

The enormous rooms were almost completely deserted and the air had the warm soft hush of old libraries. Corinne was perfectly happy, a scattering of open and closed books and papers making a semicircle around her place, as she turned the pages of the big dictionary, pen in hand, making notes.

She wrote:

Notes on the Pre-Oedipal Phase
   1. Bi-polar mood swings: rhapsody and rage (R & R). Acute pleasure of both states.
   2. Real frustration leads to state of rage; real satisfaction to rhapsody. Too simplistic?
   3. Constant sensational flux, infinite gradations of sensation, detailed specificity of the surface and interior of the body.
   4. Boundaries, thresholds, the liminal sensations. Oral, anal, genital; the gateways between inside and outside.
   5. Food and excrement prove the liminal, constitute the boundaries. Take food in, shit and piss it out. Using these membranous gateways makes sense of inside and outside.
   6. Endless hallucinogenic psychic experience. Impossible to divorce fr. bodily experience. Hypnagogic states.
   7. Things outside: source of R & R. Assoc. of colours, sounds, smells, etc. with presence/absence of M.
   8. Rage: classic wish to scratch, gouge, bite, scrape, burst, break, obliterate the body of M.
   9. Rhapsody: no division, oceanic, therefore no conflict (??) — *or* the sense of omnipotence: either all-powerful or completely frustrated. Things can't get better or worse, they're either perfect or intolerable.
   10. No boredom. (Unlike some places . . .)

Outside the celestial psychoanalytic library, Corinne was bored. You were allowed to do whatever you liked, here, even leave.

In a sense you were ignored. Occasionally Corinne suspected her research project was motivated by envy and revenge. Never having been a mother herself, she'd invented the perfect form of attack. One was supposed to have left all that behind, needless to say, but Corinne didn't want to, she held on to the thrilling intensity of the unconscious like holding on to the bar of a roller-coaster, returning again to that ecstatic, shrieking subjection.

She couldn't wait.

The Sudden Deaths of Children

Jeanie had this theory, that having children changes the terms of your relationship with death, it brings you closer to your own mortality. This is partly because of the immortality a child (possibly) promises, the sheer immortality of genes, and then there's the possibility of starting over: the kid'll do it differently, the same, that is, but better. The child both fends off death, and outlives you; it replaces you, in some sense. And partly she thought it brings you closer to death simply because the child might die. When thinking about the possibility of having a baby, Jeanie thought about the baby's death a lot.

Eventually she raised this problem with her older sister, Louise, whose son was seventeen now. Louise said, 'No, I never imagined that Paul could die, I never thought of Paul *dying*.'

Jeanie said, 'You're the most repressed person I've ever met, or maybe the most optimistic; the most well-adjusted.'

Louise said, 'Thinking about death when you think about having a baby seems a little weird to me.'

Jeanie said, 'It's logical, it's not just me being anxious — kids die *all the time*. All the time. Kids get run over *all the time*'.

'No,' Louise said, 'no, kids don't get run over all the time.'

It was hard for Jeanie to decide who was right. She knew

that kids *did* get run over, every day, and she knew too that she herself was very fearful of attachment, because any attachment always carries within it a darker implication, the risk of loss. And she envied her sister, her sister's son, with a stony, poisonous envy that burst out in the dark cry of why her not me? Even so, being terrified of possible loss, of being abandoned or bereaved, always seemed extremely logical to Jeanie. It wasn't mad. It was reasonable. She continued to anticipate the sudden deaths of children.

Jeanie made a list.

1. There was a girl at college, she was an oddball, no one liked her much; she had a sort of shadowy, slimy aspect, and she looked scared, which, since 'most everyone was in a permanent state of terror, was the one thing that was completely socially unacceptable. A story was told about this girl, that she'd killed a sibling when she was a child, she'd killed her baby brother. She was about five or six, and she'd taken the baby out of his cot or basket or baby chair, and walked onto the balcony and dropped him over the railing. We were terribly impressed. Her loneliness suddenly seemed sinister. Of course we didn't fully believe the story, but you always remembered it when you saw her cringing around the corridors.

2. I remember a little girl who tried to put the new baby in a wastepaper basket, to get rid of it. Anita's three-year-old boy was overheard by his grandmother singing little songs to himself about the new baby and riding on a train and a terrible crash where everybody dies.

3. Oliver and his partner had this baby, and Oliver's older brother and his wife, who's Italian, drove down to the

country to see the new baby, five weeks old, and they had lunch, and the new mother put the baby in her pram outside, by the kitchen door, for her nap, and the Italian sister-in-law (who had a couple of kids of her own) said, it's so cold, you English, you're so tough on the little thing, but the new mother said it was fine, and at the end of the nap suddenly the baby was completely dead, an unexplained cot death. And the mother tried to resuscitate the baby, sitting on the stairs, and then she carried her through the house, so everyone could say goodbye to the baby, and then it was over.

4. Anna's sister had a baby, a boy, and he was crying one morning and they left him, he was six months old, and then he was quiet, and then she went in and he was dead. She said she knew immediately that he was dead.

5. My cousin had a baby who pulled a chest of drawers over on herself when she was about two and a half. It killed her.

6. Sometimes babies die when they're born too early, when they're premature. That happened to Rebecca's baby.

7. Mahler wrote songs about his kids dying. I don't remember what they're called.

8. Kids get run over all the time.

On the bed: *Jeanie and Stephen were lying on the bed, talking.*

J : Do you remember that painting, it was a picture of a sky just *full* of naked babies? Spanish, seventeenth-century, eighteenth-century?

S : Yes, I think so, it was a painting of purgatory?

J : Mmm, limbo. These were all the unbaptized infants, all the untold millions of babies who die. Perinatal mortality rates in seventeenth-century Spain and the practice of baptism . . . But it must include miscarriages, and abortions — although maybe aborted babies are deemed to be little martyrs, victims —

S : — more sinned against than sinning —

J : So they get to go to heaven.

S : But in this scheme of things heaven and purgatory are very close, right? I mean, limbo — is almost as pleasant as heaven?

J : I just wonder whether the evolution of cherubs, the whole business of covering a church or a painting with millions of naked bodies of babies, is necessarily related to the infant mortality rate.

S : There *is* a difference between heaven and limbo . . .

J : Who is it that goes on about how children's bodies are the real source of pleasure for people, not sex —

S : I always thought that was crazy. I also think it's wrong — children are continually being touched by people, and it always annoys me.

J : Why?

S : It's like, after a certain stage of self-consciousness, kids can't initiate physical contact with adults (except its parents, or immediate family), but they constantly have to submit to total strangers ruffling their hair or making them smile or giving them sweets. It's like, just sitting on the bus, children are at the mercy of everyone else's desire.

J : We'd all like to be the child — the child is so beautiful, so *lovely*.

S : No, everyone wants to be the one the child loves — the one the child runs to, or responds to. We all want to have the rights of a mother, we want to take liberties.

J : It's because the child is so *sweet*.

S : Maybe *you* want to be the child, admired by everybody —

J : Yes, it must be awful, being jealous of a kid. I'm just struck, though, what a weird thing to paint. What kind of pleasure is derived from a painting of hundreds of dead babies?

S : But they're not dead, they're pink and rosy and healthy, flying around, happy as clams.

J : Surely they must remind you of your dead babies? I mean, your seventeenth-century dead babies?

S : Yes, and here they are, alive and well and living in limbo. Having a fine old time.

J : Mmm. Do you remember that church in Mexico? The one covered in babies?

S : With the babies carved in plaster.

J : That's right. It's the same sort of thing, really. Incredible *excess*, this multiplicity of interchangeable baby bodies, identically round and sweet and pink. Undifferentiated. Millions of them, millions of dead babies.

S : Jeanie, I know you insist on thinking of them as dead, but surely the whole point is that they're *not*. It's a representation of dead babies as now not dead.

J : Same difference, almost.

S : Anyway, they're angels, aren't they? Little cherubs?

J : What *is* a cherub?

S : It's a baby with wings.

J : Like a bat's a mouse with wings.

S : A rat with wings.

J : Stop!

Remembering what it was like living in a family, hell on wheels, realizing I've done everything I can to make sure this, my own house, is as different as possible, to refuse the nightmarish misunderstanding, the mistaken closeness, taking of liberties, the endless exchange of identification and projection, elaborate dance of misrecognition, the cruelty based on the false authority of adult over child, the complete lack of physical privacy, the absence of polite detachment . . . One day I came home from school and found my absolutely favourite thirties crêpe dress in a plastic washing-up bowl full of bleach. It was ruined. My mother said she had mistaken it for a rag. This I found impossible to believe. Melanie Klein says girls are terrified their mothers will destroy a) their beauty, and b) their capacity to have a baby. So why? Why, when family life is so loathsome? The intensity of biology, impelled to genetic immortality, narcissism, the logic of desire, moving on and on, always utterly wanting, always insatiable, as one thing after another disappears, unmarked, into the vast blackness of its gigantic gob . . .

An overwhelming sense of loss, when I think of how I don't see my friends, my girl friends who are married now, having babies, the women with kids. I can't bear to see them. Is this sense of loss a cover for my envy? Mourning *as always* so much easier than my conflicted feelings. I (must have) wanted to do away with the baby, to get rid of it, when it was my mother's baby, my sister's baby. I'm frightened of that — of taking the mother's place? It seems, undeniably, not for me, and at the same time, infinitely desirable. I joke with Stephen about domesticity, my persistent thoughts of the scratch on the new linoleum, my latest obsession, I say, I haven't got a baby, but I have got a *scratch*. The real woman, domesticated at last. I begin to see the absurdity of my position, and stop (for a moment) insisting that I've lost everything I could possibly want.

The child sets the seal on the narcissistic love affair. We love each other, in misrecognition, seeing you as a lovely version of myself. But the baby we produce really is a lovely version of me *and* you. It's perfect. We can adore it, even though you're jealous.

Today Stephen and I found ourselves talking about 'the baby'. 'I'd be jealous,' Stephen said, '— you'd spend all your love on *the baby*.'

'But you'd love *the baby* too,' I said.

He said, 'Yes, of course — the little *brat*.' He said it could be called Potlatch, or Robot.

I said Potlatch was OK as a middle name, perhaps. Diplomatically.

I picture us, in madonna and child mode, Stephen somehow draped at knee level, admiration of the child, or adoration, I guess, of the child on my lap.

If you allow yourself to want, something, something opens up in you, the abyss; you sense the great icy wastes of lack, a wide black sky over polar wastes, vast and desolate. You become once again the deprived child, the insecure, underprivileged, left out, lost girl and her enormous, gaping heart.

When I get a little of what I want, when I'm given a touch, a glimpse, the barest edge of love or recognition, it's like icebergs breaking up, the abyss of wanting yawns inside me, huge alligator jaws spread wide and I'm at the mercy of a yearning so vast it's impossible. I want everything.

Boa constrictors first squeeze their prey to death, surrounding their victim with coils of emotion, and then swallow it whole. This is possible because the jaw unhooks and can spread very wide. That's what I feel like: the boa constrictor about to swallow a huge animal which my violent emotion has just squeezed to death.

On the plane: *Jeanie was scared of flying. Stephen wasn't.*

J : I *hate* taking all these drugs, metronidazole, doxycycline, I hate all this chlamydia shit. I had a dream this morning, I was kneeling, crying, bare knees on cold floor, before a priest, and he says, knowing I've come to take communion (which I've never done, in real life), he says, very aggressive, 'So you have come to shoot up? It's all right,' he says, 'I shoot God too. I visit the shooting gallery. Is that what you've come for?' I didn't know the ritual phrase that you're meant to say, Father forgive me for I have sinned, I didn't know, I was crying, and he absolved me, he placed the host in my mouth — but the dream ended before I could taste it, because I've never tasted it, I guess. I woke up.

S : Sounds like a visit to the doctor.

J : Yes, but it's about babies too, about all this infertility stuff.

S : How?

J : When I was fourteen I refused to get confirmed, and my mother was furious and she said, 'Just don't ever take communion when your baby dies, when something awful happens and you need comfort!' Which of course I was very struck by, I couldn't imagine wanting to take communion in that circumstance, it seemed very foreign to me. I mean, I couldn't imagine having a baby at all, and then the idea of the baby dying seemed even more remote . . .

S : So all this fear of babies dying is fear of the malevolent, eviscerating mother, no?

J : You mean *my* mother?

S : Who wishes dead babies on you —

J : But I *chose* not to have kids, remember, and it's like Connie's mother always said, be very careful what you wish for, because you *always* get it.

S : Your wish becomes your punishment.

J : It's like a figure eight. [*Jeanie drew a figure eight with her finger on the back of the seat in front of her.*] Whatever mourning I have to do, the mourning I'm doing now for babies I maybe won't have in the future, it's like it has to *double back*, and draw in the old mourning, the old wish, that's past any possibility of restoration or salvage . . .

S : I think if you want to have a baby, we should have one.

J : I know, darling. I know.

When Jeanie was a small child, her family lived in Italy, and for her sister's eighth birthday, her parents took her to Egypt, and Jeanie was left behind. There's something fundamental about these things, about such early losses — not only *not* seeing Egypt, not only lack, but your sister so emphatically having something you don't. Nothing can ever compensate for those visions of the pyramids that she didn't see. And possibly, since her relation to Egypt existed solely on the level of fantasy, as *envy*, there's something irreducible, something very important about it. It was hers in a different way, her own to play with — to give herself (my Egypt) and to throw away (I was never taken there, I was left behind, too little). The child always envies a fantasy of something else, the child only envies what she doesn't know.

The two snapshots showed her father and Louise on a camel, and her mother on a dark horse, with robed men standing on the sand, pyramids in the background. It was 1960. She was surprised that her mother was too scared to ride a camel.

Jeanie stared at these photos with a kind of wondering disbelief: how is it possible that she, and not I, should have seen these things? These things were, inevitably, the Pyramids, the Sphinx, the Nile. Mummies. The camels, which they rode. It was like a story, unbelievable. There were camels in her ark. To ride a camel in the desert: inconceivable. The photos proved it true. That made it worse.

Her sister, Louise, upon her return, would mash together a little lump of butter and honey, to spread on her toast at breakfast. She'd learned to do this in Egypt, where they ate croissants, on a balcony, in the sun. When Jeanie tried to imitate this, to mash butter and honey, Louise was vehement, you can't do it, that's not the right way. They brought back a picture of the head of Nefertiti. Jeanie used to study the neck with pleasure.

When Jeanie grew up, she fell in love with Stephen, and he took her to Egypt.

Egypt's all about death, Jeanie thought, the frozen immobility of death, in the dry sand, dry air of the desert. Death and permanence.

The Nile valley was wet and green, and then there was a sudden line between the desert and fertility, a line where the lush green just stopped, and beyond there was only endless sand. Nothing between here and Libya, the guide said, when they visited the pyramids.

She conceived their child at the Old Cataract Hotel in Aswan, one clear morning. She enjoyed being pregnant, the companionship of this interior visitor. While the child seemed fictional at times, her body reminded her of its constant presence.

The evil eye is a look of envy; we ward it off with the image of an eye, returning the look. In Egypt, the eye is in the middle of a hand, as if the upraised hand warded off, and the look, reflected in the image of the eye, returned to the envious.

The hotel in Luxor was on an island in the Nile; there was a swimming pool, and an Arab orchestra, and a sunset arena. Jeanie sat and watched the sun set, the slow river turning gold and silver, bright green leaves merging into black, the clear sky and wide open desert in the distance. Strange birds sang. Jeanie was terribly happy.

Coda

I was perched in the little Temple of Minerva up behind the eucalyptus grove, looking down over the river and contemplating the view. I'm very fond of that temple, its delicate columns of golden stone, and the lovely bench beneath the statue. I was sitting there, thinking about the invention of the ha-ha, a grassy ditch designed to blur the division between garden and farm, a sunken fence, so that the visual transition from lawn to field is gently effected, almost imperceptible. I watched the sunlight reflecting off the silvery eucalyptus leaves below, as they shuddered slightly in the puffing wind. The transition, from inside to outside, that the ha-ha visually dissolves, is less symbolically pressing here, where Nature is never inclement or malign. Still, you don't want the sheep to eat the peonies, do you?

Corinne appeared, stepping quietly through the columns of the little round temple. I was pleased to see her.

'My dear, you're back. It seems like only a moment since —'

'It *was* rather a short life.'

'Do tell.'

'Well, you remember how I was trying to persuade them to let me do an experiment . . . It was only because I was proposing to stay just a short while that they let me go through with it.'

'That's marvellous, you actually succeeded in cutting through all that mysterious red tape — it's simply marvellous.'

'I wanted to see what existence would be like if you never got past that first attachment, you know, if you never had to give the mother up.'

'But that's absurd —'

'I know, that's what everyone thinks. That consciousness and language and the whole structure of the psyche only come into being *through* that process of giving the mother up, and coping with the father's threat. Insofar as the pre-oedipal phase exists at all, it seems to be retrospective, something that only comes into awareness just at the moment you lose it forever. They think consciousness sounds the deathknell of that early relationship, it only exists as loss.'

'You spend far too much time in the libraries of psychoanalysis. Really, conditions of existence are much better described in philosophy.'

'But I wanted to test this theory out — by dying before I ever reached the oedipal phase. So it couldn't be retrospectively determined.'

'And?'

'It's all nonsense. Admittedly, I didn't acquire language, or

gender, or a sense of identity, but I was aware all the time, of
everything around me. Maybe it's not consciousness, maybe it's
a different kind of awareness. One that consciousness makes
you forget.'

'What were you aware of?'

'I could feel all my internal organs, I could feel the blood in
my veins, and my heart pumping, and my gut digesting. It was
very preoccupying, these sensations, I found it hard to focus
on the outside world.'

'Hang on a second, how old were you?'

'I killed myself when I was six months old.'

'This is extraordinary. How?'

'I stopped breathing. It's quite common. You just, so to
speak, forget to breathe.'

'I'm deeply shocked. And you spent most of the time listening to your peristaltic waves?'

'Feeling them, feeling everything going on inside me in the
most amazing detail. And being with, or without, the mother.'

'And the father?'

'He was peripheral, when he wasn't absent. I wasn't bothered.
I never made the connection that *he* was taking the mother
away. Or that anyone was. Her absence seemed like a tragic act
of fate, completely non-negotiable. Although I protested, of
course. Rage is very pleasurable.'

'And the mother?'

'Jeanie? I think she'll get over it. She'd predicted it anyway,
she was always frightened her baby would die.'

'Is that why you chose her?'

'In a sense she was prepared for it. More prepared than most.'

'I think this is the most sadistic piece of sublunary research
I've ever come across. I thought when you said you wanted to
go back, to walk those chaotic, dirty streets —'

'In my mother's belly. I wanted to be inside her, and to
know, somewhere deep in my bones, that this was it, there
wasn't going to be anything more than this. The first love, and
no other.'

'And now?'

'Now I'm working on promotion to angel status.'

'So you can interfere even more?'

'So I can communicate some of my discoveries. Being a baby is an awareness before division, before anything is divided up: sleep and waking, sexual sensations and others, thinking and feeling, inner and outer, pleasure and pain. The whole surface of my body, the dark volume inside me, were constantly surging with sensation, like perpetual electricity, pins and needles, but pleasurable. It's really great.'

'That's why babies scream so much.'

'That's the other side, you're at the mercy of things, not only beyond your control, but beyond you in every sense. Pure pain, no understanding.'

'None of this seems very original to me, it's rather what I imagined infancy would be like.'

'Yes, me too. But this is scientific.'

'Rubbish. Corinne, you really are a disappointment.'

'Don't be horrible to me.'

'I'm sorry, my dear. I forgot you've never had a child of your own. It may be youthful high spirits, I suppose, and curiosity, but I think it's very cruel to those poor parents of yours . . .'

'You're a sentimentalist.'

'I like the eighteenth century. Sentimental wasn't a dirty word in the eighteenth century.'

'And scientific isn't a dirty word now.'

'I don't call it science. I call it revenge.'

'Possibly a combination of envy and revenge. But all science has an unconscious motivation.'

'Enough of this. Let's walk down to the lake and look at the pyramids.'

'All right.'

Generosity

Every Indian or other person who engages in or assists in celebrating or encourages either directly or indirectly another to celebrate any Indian festival, dance or other ceremony of which the giving away or paying or giving back of money, goods or articles of any sort forms a part or is a feature, whether such gift of money, goods or articles takes place before, at or after the celebration of the same, or who encourages or assists in any celebration or dance of which the wounding or mutilation of the dead or living body of any human being or animal forms a part or is a feature, is guilty of an offense and is liable on summary conviction for a term not exceeding six months and not less than two months.

Revised Statutes of Canada, 1927,
Vol. II, Ch. 98, no. 140, p. 2218

Potlatch was first banned by Canadian law in 1884, but this was rarely enforced, partly because the wording of the statute was too vague, and partly because the local magistrate and officials had a relatively tolerant attitude. It stopped completely only during World War I, when the Kwakiutl were instructed by the government agent, 'not to enjoy ourselves while the war was on. We all agree to do as he told us. And had no Potlatch as long as the war was on. And when the war was through we started again.'

Prosecutions followed. Charlie Nowell was sentenced to three months in gaol for giving money to people who came to his brother's funeral. An Indian delegation to Ottawa made no impact. In 1919, in a dramatic courtroom scene, the four accused, as well as seventy-five other men present, agreed to give up the potlatch. In return, the four were given suspended sentences by the government agent, in his role as magistrate and judge. He was aware that sending heads of households to gaol would only produce more families dependent on Indian Agency hand-outs, and no doubt this influenced his decision.

By 1921, the agent was confident that things were once again under control. However, late in the year several more potlatches took place, and then at Christmas he heard about what was rumoured to be the biggest potlatch ever held in the agency. This was Dan Cranmer's potlatch, the 'Christmas Tree' potlatch, which took place at Village Island in Alert Bay. Douglas Cole writes: 'It lasted six days, and involved the giving away of thousands of dollars worth of motor boats, pool tables, sewing machines, gramophones, blankets, flour, and cash.' The local Mounties closed the potlatch down. Twenty-nine Indians, shopped by two who had themselves taken part in the Cranmer potlatch, were prosecuted. The Indians pleaded guilty, and counsel asked for suspended sentences on the grounds that the accused would agree to abstain from potlatch forever.

The Royal Canadian Mounted Police constable objected, pointing out that some of the accused were the very people who'd promised to give up the potlatch in 1919. He insisted on tangible evidence of their reformation, and suggested that the only convincing evidence that was in their power to provide was to 'make a voluntary surrender of all "Potlach" coppers, masks, head dresses, Potlach blankets and boxes and all other parpfanalia used solely for Potlach purposes.' Some of the bands agreed to these terms: The Lekwiltok of Cape Mudge, the Mamalillikulla of Village Island, and the Nimkish of Alert Bay. The people of Turnour Island and Fort Rupert resisted, however, with the result that many of them were sent to prison, including several women, among them a grandmother.

The surrendered potlatch paraphernalia was collected in a woodshed, and then moved to the parish hall in Alert Bay, where it was put on display. It amounted to more than 450 items, including 'twenty coppers, scores of Hamatsa whistles, and dozens of masks'. The government agent wrote: 'It should command good prices for museum purposes.' He was supposed to send it straight to the National Museum in Ottawa, but there was a delay of several months in packing the various things into crates. Meanwhile, in September 1922, G. W. Heye, one of the most notorious collectors of Indian artefacts, rolled into town, and asked to see the collection. The agent sold Heye thirty-five of the best pieces for $291.

The Department of Indian Affairs and the National Museum were outraged when they heard about the sale, especially since the pieces were to be exported to the United States and placed in the Museum of the American Indian, which Heye had founded in 1916. Since the articles were now 'beyond recall', however, they decided to let the matter rest. The remaining material was shipped in seventeen cases to Ottawa, where the appraisal, made by the anthropologist, Edward Sapir, excluding the coppers, came to $1,456. The Indians considered the compensation 'entirely inadequate'. Masks were valued at two to ten dollars (Heye had paid twenty-five for his), and Hamatsa whistles were deemed worth one dollar only. The ceremonial shields, or coppers, were more problematic. Made simply from sheets of copper, each was endowed with its own heraldic pedigree and ritual power, its own soul, so to speak. The value of the coppers was symbolic, or artificial, purely a result of ritual exchange within the social and ceremonial system of Kwakiutl culture. It was impossible, therefore, to estimate an objective monetary value for them. As a result, no compensation was ever paid.

It seems likely that those Indians who cooperated with the police and surrendered various ceremonial items did not hand over everything they owned. The Mounties tactfully refrained from searching people's houses. George Hunt, who worked for many years with the anthropologist Franz Boas, often played the part of middle man between the two communities. (His father was English and had been the Hudson's Bay Company factor at Fort Rupert, and although his mother was a Tlingit, Hunt was raised as a Kwakiutl.) Hunt was employed by Sapir to investigate the genealogy of the surrendered coppers, and he uncovered evidence of a simple sleight-of-hand. While at Kingcombe, he heard that Bob Robertson, owner of the great Loch copper, was telling people that he'd given a facsimile of the Loch to the police, and kept the real thing for himself.

After many years, the coppers came back. In 1979 and 1980, as the outcome of prolonged negotiations, the National Museum in Ottawa, where the collection had remained relatively intact, agreed to return the material to suitable museums established by the Indian communities of Alert Bay and Cape Mudge. It was the first such transfer of this kind.

The thirty-five objects G. W. Heye purchased for the Museum of the American Indian had a curious history. During the 1940s, many pieces from his vast collection of Northwest Coast artefacts were sold by Heye to the Surrealists, then refugees in New York. Max Ernst, André Breton, Matta, Tanguy, and others, including their friend Lévi-Strauss, became enthusiastic collectors of this work, and Heye, in his position as both founder and director of the Museum, had no qualms about disposing of the very pieces he had so fervently pursued on numerous personal expeditions to the Northwest.

The Surrealists were allowed to browse at their leisure through the vast warehouses of the Museum, located in the Bronx, where the endless shelves and crates loaded with masks and carvings and button blankets called to mind the great potlatches of former times. Heye himself, the bargain hunter *par excellence*, let them have the pieces they selected at cut-rate, not to say giveaway, prices. Thus we see how Kwakiutl masks, confiscated by the Canadian courts, may end up on the living-room walls of Paris intellectuals.

A long time after the diaries incident, maybe two years, Carrie ran into Howard in the street. He was thin and tall, not angular but bowed rather, bending over her slightly as he spoke. Howard showed Carrie his wrist, bony and pale, circled by a bracelet of bright red cotton, knotted simply. He said, 'It's protection: someone's been trying to steal my soul.' Carrie replied, 'It was me. Aeons ago.' He was shocked.

It was when they first met, when she cast that spell, when she was sixteen, and still living with her mother. They'd met before, in London, with the 'gang', when she was fourteen or so; he'd been fat then, a pale and moon-like face, and he carried with him a small pink toy mouse called Sleep. Everyone had toys or gimmicks, conversation pieces, in those days. She used to carry a metal lunchbox, full of tricks. But this was later, in Ireland, at Sally's house, when they met again, and she fell in love.

Carrie'd wanted to fall in love, she was on the lookout for a suitable object. She'd even written in the diary the week before, 'I wonder if I'll fall in love with Howard when he comes' — inky evidence of the inauthenticity of her fall. It was complete.

Time passed, and Carrie was in love; she and Howard would stay up all night together, and go out to watch the sun come up over Hampstead Heath, and spend endless afternoons listening to music, smoking dope, hanging out. Clambering over the park railings at four a.m., to wake up the ducks at dawn in St James Park, she felt invincible. Paralysed with love, Carrie passed days, and nights, silent, by his side, hoping for a little more. But nothing ever happened.

Meanwhile Carrie was going to school every day, hating her teachers, getting into trouble, bunking off, and compulsively talking to her friends. Schoolgirls still, the elaborate vocabulary of adolescent romance was called upon to make sense of their all too serious love affairs. It was around this time that she made friends with Jo. Compulsive, she spoke of him, an incessant interpretation of incidents, hearsay, phone calls, constantly going over the evidence to produce an answer to one question: does he love me? Jo listened, taking it all in. Carrie told stories, as if a line, a rope, a sequence could hold it all, could account for this emotional turmoil. Jo, self-contained, kept her thoughts and feelings close, planted like seeds. Carrie was scattered and desperate, and then suddenly quiet when she was with him.

Carrie was reading Frazer's *Golden Bough*, more or less because she wanted to understand Eliot, and Modernism, and late one night she found a spell. It was a spell to be performed under a red moon, in Malaya, by those who want their love returned. Carrie was sitting crouched on her narrow bed, in the little attic room she lived in at the top of her mother's house. There was a very large Beardsley poster on the wall beside the bed, and over her head, as a wry comment on her virginity, she'd stuck a *News of the World* placard, a crude banner headline that read: MY WILD NIGHTS WITH THE MAD AXEMAN.

Next door to her white room was a narrow bathroom, with a small casement window that opened onto a parapet. If you were willing to risk death, a drop of five storeys, it was possible to clamber out of the bathroom window, and step from the parapet diagonally across onto the small flat roof of the back extension. The July night that Carrie was reading *The Golden Bough*, as she got to the bit about soul-catching, and the red moon low over the eastern horizon, she looked out of the window and saw, for the first time in this city, a huge fat red moon, lying low in the dark sky. Without hesitation, she carefully re-read the spell, and got up off the bed to climb out of the bathroom window onto the roof. She had never before carried out this delicate operation at night. The red full moon was uncanny, an unexpected gift.

Holding the thick paperback in her hands, her long hair falling down her back, face turned up towards the moon, Carrie repeated the words, following the directions 'for securing the soul of one whom you wish to render distraught'.

I loose my shaft, I loose it and the moon clouds over,
I loose it, and the sun is extinguished.
I loose it, and the stars burn dim.
But it is not the sun, moon, and stars that I shoot at,
It is the stalk of the heart of that child, So-and-so.

Cluck! cluck! soul of So-and-so, come and walk with me.
Come and sit with me,
Come and sleep and share my pillow.
Cluck! cluck! soul.

Somebody at sunrise be distraught for love of me,
Somebody at sunset be distraught for love of me,
As you remember your parents, remember me;
As you remember your house and house-ladder,
    remember me;
When thunder rumbles, remember me;
When wind whistles, remember me;
When the heavens rain, remember me;
When the cocks crow, remember me;
When you look up at the sun, remember me;
When you look up at the moon, remember me;

For in that self-same moon I am there.
Cluck! cluck! soul of Somebody come hither to me.
I do not mean to let you have my soul,
Let your soul come hither to mine.

The spell worked. Only a few weeks later, he took her hand and kissed it, sitting on the floor at her feet very late at night, and she leaned forward, bending down over his upturned face, to kiss his lips. Months passed; in his bookshelf, Carrie found the very same edition of *The Golden Bough*, a fat paperback with its spine uncreased, and she wrote his initials HWS in fine pencil in the margin beside the spell. She wanted to be found out, some day; it was a dead giveaway.

In the street, all these years later, Howard looked at her with mild horror. Carrie thought, he's been to India now, he's finally getting around to reading Frazer. Howard explained how he'd found the counter-spell, the red thread tied around the wrist, in the same chapter. 'Jo said she thought it was you,' he muttered.

Carrie laughed, defiant, at last: 'She was right!'

Carrie remembered Jo on the beach, in Dorset, taking off her clothes to go swimming and expressing with annoyance how clumsy she felt, how uncomfortable she was, undressed. She was seventeen, then. Jo was beautiful, she had a kind of pent-up fierceness inside her, that emerged in gestures of irritation or dismissal. Her face was like a Spanish saint. Her hand, moving, would convey the aggression her body contained; she stood firm on the ground, immovable, like a heifer, or a young bull.

Carrie remembered another time, a couple of years later, Jo asking her, suddenly, 'Do you have orgasms?' She'd been a little shaken, and answered yes, automatically. It turned out Jo didn't, with Howard, and wondered if Carrie did, or had.

'No, not with Howard.'

'When, then?'

'Well, masturbating . . .'

'Oh,' Jo said, her hands making a gesture of dismissal, 'masturbation's not a problem.' She produced a leaflet called *The Myth of the Vaginal Orgasm*, and Carrie read it, amazed. She'd never talked about this stuff before.

Later Howard worked it into his stand-up comedy routine; he'd sing a song, in the persona of a rather lame new man type, about a meaningful relationship where he went out with a woman for four years and she never had an orgasm. The audience roared. Howard became a famous comedian, eventually; she'd see him on TV occasionally, by chance.

Much later, in New York, Carrie found herself in a half-empty movie theatre one afternoon, watching *Brazil*, with her friend Louise. Without warning, Howard appeared on the screen, momentarily, for one short gag, just time for Carrie to point and cry out, '*That*'s the first man I ever slept with!'

'Which one?'

'Him! Him! There!' she shrieked, whispering, while the rest of the scattered audience started to rustle and snicker.

Finally, something like twelve or fifteen years later, she saw Jo across a crowded room at an opening at the Hayward, and at first she thought Jo was cutting her. This was intolerable, so Carrie went up to say hello. Bill was standing next to her. Carrie said, warmly, 'I hear you've had a baby, congratulations!' And Jo pointed to her stomach and said, 'Another one on the way.' Laughing, Carrie said, 'Oh I'm envious, I want one of them.' Whereupon Jo looked hard at her and said, dubiously, 'Why would *you* want to have a baby?' That did it, finally. Looking at Jo, her attachment unfolded, turning inside out. Carrie had nothing to say.

The night he told her, the night he illuminated her darkness, untied the knots of confusion, exposing a landscape of utter devastation, that night was seared into Carrie's mind, burned into her like blinding flares slow falling in a black sky.

In the morning Howard called her up, asked her over, to spend the day. This hadn't happened in a very long time. (Later, she would realize that Jo must have put him up to it, she must have said, 'You have to tell her. She doesn't know, she hasn't guessed. You have to tell her this weekend.') Carrie was terribly pleased that he'd called, that he'd pursued her, for once. He was living in Oxford, going to college, and she was still at school in London, that was one reason they didn't see each other much. Lately, however, when they spent time together, Jo was there, or other people, his younger brother's friends, and things were strained and difficult. Typically Carrie didn't question this; she imagined the strain must somehow be her fault, that she wasn't pleasing him in some way. She hoped it would go away, hoping like holding your breath and closing your eyes and wishing this unpleasure would somehow fade. The ostrich position? Meanwhile, she stayed quiet, keeping her head down, so she wouldn't have to see, she wouldn't have to feel the slap in the face.

She never questioned this, accepting it all as part of being in love, the price of being allowed to spend time with him. It was as if she had no rights, no claim on anyone, no expectations. She couldn't say, 'Don't treat me this way.' One time she worked up her courage to telephone and she dialled his number and laughing he told her that Jo was there and they were pretending it was a power cut (it was a winter of power cuts, the miners were bringing the Tory government down, people took baths by candlelight and talked about how it was like Dickens), that evening Jo and Howard were pretending, they were lighting candles together, playing at power cuts. Carrie winced inside, unable even to acknowledge it to herself. She was scared to death, and didn't know it.

That day, the day Howard called, Saturday, Carrie put on a red dress, and she washed her hair, and then she got on the bus for the long ride to his house, his parents' house. It was sunny, mid-February, a clear cold day with the pale sunlight of English winters. She was friendly with his mother, who was also called

Carrie. That day, his mother was particularly sweet to her, and
Howard became impatient. They went out, Hampstead Heath
was nearby, and they went there, as they always did. He was so
nice to her, talking and paying attention to her only. Carrie
was quietly ecstatic. She was used to doing whatever he wanted
her to do, appearing when he asked her to, going home when
he wanted her to leave, fucking him, or not, as he chose. She
accepted this lavish attention now with silent amazement, it
seemed an unlooked-for gift from the gods.

They sat on the low bough of an ancient tree, and he told
her how he had a weapon against her, there was something he
had to tell her, he had this weapon against her and he had to
give it up. Carrie insisted on remaining completely oblivious
to this threat. She wasn't curious, she affected a profound
detachment from such unpleasantness. Idealistic, she didn't want
to know. She kept saying, 'Forget it, don't worry about it. It's
such a lovely day, don't ruin it.' And he went on clutching his
head and saying, 'There's something I have to tell you.' And
she kept smiling gently and floating airily through the park,
saying, 'Stop worrying, forget it.'

In this way the whole day passed, until finally, late at night,
they went back to her place, to climb into her narrow bed with
the bright yellow sheets and make love once more. It was two
in the morning when he finally said it, when he finally managed
to say the fatal words: 'There's someone else.' Later Carrie
figured he must have promised himself, or Jo, that he'd tell her
before the day was out; cowardly, he'd left it to the last possible
minute, so late at night, and really a lousy moment, post-coital,
but at least he managed to get the words out of his mouth.

Her first response was to sustain her pose of total disinterest,
airy detachment. She immediately envisaged the Other Woman,
a blonde girl called something like Diane, or Suzette, even, a
blonde with painted fingernails and eye makeup. It was a vision
of everything she wasn't, a cliché of sexiness against which she,
Carrie, could play soulmate. Carrie's implicit, unspoken line
on this was: 'I can take anything you've got to give, nothing

you can do or say can change my love for you, and while you're at it, please don't drag me into the ghastly details of your little peccadilloes, please, my love for you is far far above all this.'

So at first she said nothing, lying flat on her back naked in the narrow bed, so close to his long body. Her eyes were focused on nothing, some point in the middle distance above her head. He said, 'There's someone else.' She said nothing. She absented herself from this conversation. It was a pretty effective tactic, she could see that it upset him. He pressed her, he said, 'You have to help me, please, help me to tell you. I've got to tell you. Please, ask me questions.' Submissive in all things, Carrie did not speak her mind (she really didn't want to know), instead she lay there and tried to think of a question to ask. There was nothing she wanted to know. She thought of the most innocuous, least informative question she could ask, a question that took it for granted that she'd never met this other woman. She said, 'OK. What's her name?' Howard hesitated, then he said, 'You know.'

Shock flooded her body, like a bright light suddenly switched on. It was Jo, of course, and suddenly everything made sense. Carrie was shocked to the bone. She wanted to talk to her right away. It was too late at night to phone. Somewhere she had always known, yet she'd never suspected, even remotely. Carrie had nothing whatsoever to say to Howard. She felt this was between her and Jo, Howard was irrelevant, almost, or unimportant. She didn't want to talk about it with him, she didn't really want to have anything to do with him. She'd never told him how much she loved him, she'd hidden all that, absolutely certain the ludicrous extent of her adoration would be totally unacceptable. He didn't know what he'd done. But Jo knew. Carrie had told Jo everything.

As the night passed it became clear that Howard seemed to think they could go on as before, that the problem had been Carrie's innocence, or ignorance, her terrible vulnerability. He didn't want to have to choose between them. That was intolerable to him. He refused his position of power. He didn't want to hurt her, or Jo, he didn't want to stop seeing either of them. They were free. Eyes open wide, Carrie still had nothing to say. The one she wanted to talk to was Jo. She was reeling from the double shock: the sexual betrayal, the humiliating realization of her own blindness. There was nothing left. She didn't sleep very well.

In the morning she rang Jo as early as possible. She said 'Please come round. I want to talk to you.' Jo gave out a sort of shrieking giggle, most uncharacteristic, and Carrie realized with surprise that Jo must be nervous, even scared of her. Carrie was playing to an internal audience, it was epic operatic tragic drama she was enacting, and they were nervous? This was annoying. Carrie felt that she was rising to the occasion, so to speak, or maybe dragging the somewhat paltry and banal occasion up closer to her high ideals. She hoped Jo and Howard wouldn't let her down.

What happened then was Howard wouldn't leave. He understood that Jo was coming round, to talk to Carrie, and he wouldn't leave. He hung around, playing the guitar. Carrie was distraught, silent, even beginning to feel glimmers of anger. Finally she asked him to go. He stayed. Later she guessed or recognized that he was madly in love with Jo, and thus compelled perhaps to take every chance of a few moments with her. She was perplexed. Then there was the horrible possibility that Jo had arranged this with him, fixed it so that she, Jo, wouldn't be left alone with Carrie's possible wrath. Carrie felt nauseous.

Eventually, Jo appeared, nervous, and like lovers do, their eyes locked, Jo and Howard sat down close together, they couldn't resist touching each other, and they ignored Carrie. Maybe they really were scared of her, of what she'd say. Or maybe this was the moment of truth, representing some kind of commitment to this until now more or less illicit or undercover romance. Calculating back to the evening in Richmond when Jo told Carrie she was thinking of going on the pill, and wouldn't say why, Carrie guessed they'd been sleeping together for about two and a half months. Carrie sensed they were protecting themselves against her, and she felt upset that she should seem so threatening, when she was the one who'd been wronged. They even looked alike, Howard and Jo: pale skin, dark hair, long narrow eyes.

Again, Carrie asked Howard to go. He left, reluctantly. Possibly he was squeamish about what these two would say about him now that they both knew what he'd been doing, what they'd say behind his back. Carrie didn't care, that wasn't the issue. The issue for Carrie was straightforward: how could Jo keep her in the dark for so long?

Years later, it was the fried eggs she remembered, the eggs she fried to give to Jo and Howard the morning Jo got back from the States. Carrie had been lying in bed with Howard that morning, his long, pale body, warm skin so close in the big bed. She'd been lying in his arms, her ex-boyfriend's arms, where she wanted to be, when the doorbell rang, too early in the morning. (She'd moved out of her mother's house, by then, she was living with her sister, Tina.) Carrie had no recollection of throwing a dressing-gown on, walking barefoot down the icy hall to the front door, only the unspeakable shock when the door opened to reveal Jo — Jo back, unannounced, unexpected — Jo, straight from the airport, with some guy in tow, a bearded hippy she'd met on the plane.

They'd come straight from the airport; the hippy was coming down off acid; but none of this registered, what registered was the (mistaken) idea that Jo had come to Carrie's house because she (inexplicably) knew Howard was there. Carrie didn't question this idea (it made no sense), later she realized it was because she felt bad about sleeping with Howard while Jo was away. Despite everything, Carrie insisted on continuing to think of Jo as one of her dearest friends. She'd given them her blessing, she'd given up, and therefore she felt she really shouldn't fall into bed with Howard when Jo wasn't around. Nevertheless, when Howard came after her, when he came knocking on her door late at night, unannounced, unexpected, after Jo left for the States, Carrie would take him gladly into her bed, wrap her smooth body around him, and feel badly, a horrible little black scrap of bad feeling, about Jo.

So it was frighteningly appropriate, that on one of these mornings (he only slept with her three or maybe four times in the three weeks Jo was away, although once he showed up when she was in bed with Jo's brother, Philip, and maybe he would have stayed the night if she hadn't been), on one of these blissful mornings of re-possession, with Howard still asleep in the big bed, it seemed almost appropriate that Carrie should open the door and find Jo. And believe, unquestioning, that Jo knew Howard was there.

There was a moment of pure confusion, when it became clear that Jo didn't know. Carrie remembered the tiny contortions of her face, as Jo took in the fact that he was here, that Carrie thought she knew he was here and, implicitly, that Carrie had probably been lying in bed with him only moments before. All this took place on the doorstep, and then Jo, decisive, moved directly down the corridor to the bedroom, while Carrie showed the tripping hippy to the floor cushions in the front room, and asked him if he wanted anything, some orange juice, or what. He wanted to crash out.

She went back down the hall, and saw Jo, radiantly happy, clambering into the bed, with her clothes on, and Howard, also looking completely blissed out, kissing her shoulder, gently, looking like he always did when he woke up, bemused and wondering.

Carrie's automatic response to this unspeakably painful scene was to worry that Jo might be hurt or upset, might think she'd been sleeping with Howard. It was her sister's bed, the big bed (Tina was away) that Howard was lying naked in, and just conceivably Carrie might have slept in her own bed, the bed in the front room, and put Howard in the big bed, if he'd come round then stayed too late to drive home. Anxious, Carrie wanted to protect Jo from realizing what had happened; she hoped she wouldn't notice the two pillows, side by side, the dent she'd left in her sleep. Carrie almost succeeded in thinking she was pleased to see Jo, pleased to see the two of them so happy. The only thing she wasn't quite up for was the hippy stranger, sprawled across the floor cushions, sound asleep.

So she had no place to be; there were only two rooms in this flat, the bedroom at the back, and the front room, her room, where she usually slept; Carrie had no place to be, so she decided to make breakfast. She vanished into the very small kitchen. She fried two eggs, in butter. They were pale and smooth, without colour, and she put them on a large white plate, alone. She didn't make toast; they were out of bread.

She took this flat white plate with its shiny flat white eggs into the bedroom, the fried eggs sliding slightly on the surface of the plate, she took them in to give to Howard and Jo. They looked up at her from their absorbed embrace, eyes locked in passionate rediscovery, they looked up at her, distractedly, as if surprised that anyone else existed in the world. She gave them the plate with the two eggs on it, and two forks, recognizing for the first time that this breakfast really wasn't very appetizing. It was more like a gesture, this gift, a representation of a good breakfast: eggs. Really it wasn't very nice. Carrie retreated once more, leaving them to it.

She opened the french windows that led from the front room down the side of the house to the garden at the back, and sat down on the step, her elbows propped on her knees, holding her head. It was wearing, this; she felt worn out. A while later the hippy surfaced and volunteered the information that tripping out on long flights was really the best place to do acid because he'd realized the only real problem, on acid, was having to make decisions. And on a plane, there are no decisions to make. You just sit in your seat for eight hours. Eliminate alternatives to avoid a bad trip.

Carrie had so far successfully managed to avoid all hallucino-genic drugs, despite the fact that almost everyone she knew dropped acid regularly. Nevertheless, she harboured a soft spot for the fantasy of tripping out on pure organic mescalin, some day, in nature, in a lovely park on a sunny day, some time. The idea of doing acid inside the plastic environment of a trans-atlantic jet was completely uncongenial to her. She hated flying anyway. What if you did have a bad trip? There would be nowhere to go. Hell. Stuck in a nightmare. Not so very dissimi-lar to the predicament she found herself in now.

I think I've forgotten everything I knew about potlatch. I always forget. I can't even remember the plot of a novel unless I've read it nineteen times. I read all those potlatch books last year and they all started to merge into each other.

The one I liked best wasn't really about potlatch at all. It was about this man called William Duncan of Metlakatla, Metlakatla was the utopian community he founded. He was a missionary, from England, Lincolnshire, I think, working-class background, mid-nineteenth century, he was an apprentice, and he read all these improve yourself books, anyway, eventually he became a missionary and was sent out to British Columbia to save the Indians, the Tsimshian. And what was so annoying and perplexing to all the British missionaries and the upright proper merchants and all the colonialists, was what a fine old time the Indians in BC were having without having to do any of what they would call real work. The whole ethic of work and save and suffer and pray and die and go to heaven, the whole thing was completely irrelevant to these people. They were rich, they lived well, they always had plenty to eat, endless salmon and oolachan, and lots of leisure time, so an enormous part of their culture was about games and rituals, literally think-ing up things to do in the winter months when the snows came. Even war for them was a kind of huge game, all revolving around the question of status. It was all about showing off.

So the big problem the missionaries faced was how to persuade these people to give up this rather pleasant life, to abandon their extremely elaborate mythology and religion and structures of ritual and family and everything, to make them so to speak buckle under and face the fact that we're put here on earth to suffer, and Jesus died for our sins, and the wages of sin is death, and we're all going to die. All that. And work, they had to make them work. And live in separate houses — the Kwakiutl and the Tsimshian and the Haida all lived in big wooden houses, beautifully painted, thirty or forty people in each, and these buildings were really ideal for the constant parties and elaborate plays and performances and all the socializing they went in for. And the potlatch. Most of all, they had to stop the potlatch. It was the key issue really, to get them to accept a (literally) capitalist economy, an economy of saving and investment and labour and just rewards in heaven, to get them to stop giving everything away! Anyway, William Duncan tried and tried, and also of course there was the struggle against liquor and prostitution and all the sinful activity that contact with the Europeans introduced. Particularly alcohol.

Eventually Duncan realized that the only way to get them to forsake their culture, and to protect them from the temptations of the local fort, was to remove them from it entirely, i.e. to build a new village, where everything would be organized along Christian principles. Where he would be the sole arbiter of Christian economics and moral behaviour. He was greatly helped in this project by a massive smallpox epidemic that swept through the Indian communities, moving north up the coast from Victoria, wiping out thousands — many of them, it goes without saying, already considerably weakened by venereal disease which they'd acquired through prostituting the women in Victoria and Prince Rupert and Fort Simpson. Needless to say, Duncan had no hesitation in depicting this epidemic as a scourge from heaven, and lots of lost people were recruited to the new village out of sheer desperation and grief. Maybe a few hundred, to begin with; there were almost a thousand at its height.

And they set off and built Metlakatla, the city on the hill, and William Duncan ruled it like an absolute monarch, making up rules and regulations and punishments, the carrot and the stick, to cajole and enforce his ideas of propriety. After a few years there was gossip in Victoria that he was fucking the young women, and certainly it was true that he beat them severely for relatively minor misdemeanours. He used to lock them up in the cupboard under the stairs.

By this time he wasn't on good terms with the Anglican church establishment in Canada or England, nor with the Missionary Society. And there was some fracas, another church-man appeared, he sneaked in while William Duncan was away, and he gave a rousing sermon on the mystic powers of the Holy Ghost, whereupon the Metlakatla people started having visions and seeing signs, and crying out in frenzy, and a bunch of them stayed up all night praying and heard the voice of the Holy Spirit itself. And Duncan heard about this down in Victoria, and he hightailed it back up to Metlakatla, which was pretty remote, and then basically he punished these people for days until they finally admitted that their visions and aural hallucinations (which of course were particularly dangerous because they weren't so very different from the kind of ecstatic states Duncan associated with their own religion), these visions were a snare and a delusion, and the work of the devil, and it was back to the Duncan line on all of this, which was pretty fucking minimal. Like for example, Duncan never let them celebrate communion, he never told them about it, transubstantiation, because it was too close to their religion. It was as if he wanted to abolish all traces of metaphor, and any kind of extreme spiritual state, and all rituals of performance, to distance the Anglican church as much as possible from the Winter Dances and the great potlatches of former times. On the other hand, he let them put up carved totem poles on either side of the altar in one of the chapels. So it wasn't simple.

What was interesting about Metlakatla was this kind of compromise, in all the practical stuff, like what to wear. It's always the same problem for these missionaries: how to get people to give up their comfortable and efficient clothes, for uncomfortable and inefficient and expensive European dress. And the problem of architecture, to get them to give up their communal houses. They came to a compromise on the houses by sort of shoving the two styles together. They'd build two conventional Anglo-style houses, with two storeys, and separate rooms, etc., and then on the ground floor a great room to connect the two houses, with a fire burning in it, so you could still hang out together, in one great long smoky room. But you slept in a proper, private space.

Also Duncan was very business-minded, and into manufacturing whatever there was a market for, including tourist artefacts. They all did it, all the different bands made stuff to sell to the foreigners, from really early on, but it was particularly striking at Metlakatla because they'd made such an effort to impose European standards of dress and cleanliness and punctuality and privacy. And then years pass and Duncan is getting the old women to teach the young women how to make the traditional head-dresses out of bark, so that he can sell them down at Fort Simpson. Getting them to remember the things he'd tried so hard to make them forget.

I don't remember it very clearly. I know it was dark, when they came, it was late, and I think they telephoned first, I think it was Jo on the phone, saying, 'We want to come round, is that all right?' And of course I said yes, because I said yes to everything, it was the easiest thing to do. Or maybe I said yes because I wanted to see them, to see him, to see her. I don't know. I was going to school every day, they weren't. By that time Howard was dropping out of college, and Jo hadn't started yet, she was doing her ritual year off before university, the year in which you were meant to travel, to hitch around the US, or take the overland route to India.

In any case I remember it was dark when they came, and I guess I was alone, I don't know where Tina was, maybe she was out, I don't know. It wasn't very long after the whole débâcle, the extraordinary renunciation I'd made, this moment when I'd broken the triangle, I'd said, 'Oh OK, go.' I'd said, 'I don't want to play any more.' I'd said, 'He's all yours.' Somehow during this time I'd salvaged something from the wreckage, an image of myself, some kind of narrative in which I starred, pale and wan, the classic victim of a broken heart, magnanimously giving up the man she loves to the woman who's betrayed her. See, I could have fought for him; I could at least have made their lives a misery. I could have made bitter accusations. But I didn't. I was proud, I was generous, and I behaved impeccably.

Anyway it wasn't very long after all this drama, and we were all three of us busy fervently pretending that there wasn't a problem, that we could still continue to be friends. At least that's what I was doing. So I was slightly surprised to find how much tension there was when they walked in, when they entered this little front room where we'd all spent so much time separately and together, where the love affair had taken place and where my heart had been broken. They came in, and I do remember that they didn't seem to find it easy to be together in front of me, which I guess isn't that surprising, but still I think that was more Howard than Jo, Jo wanted things to be clear, I think, whereas Howard felt guilty and also perhaps he wanted me still. I don't know. I mean, when she went to the States he used to come and sleep with me, I didn't know what that was about. I liked it though, sleeping with him, I mean fucking him, and sleeping with him. I was in love with him still, I guess.

So anyway that night they weren't really very much at ease, you know, and neither was I, but I was always taking up this position of fearlessness, I think it was my mother's training, I could always pull it out of the hat, this sort of social ease, this savoir-faire. In any case, I was able to seem more at ease than they were, although I'm sure I was in crisis inside. And so they didn't sit down or anything like that, I remember Howard sort of wandered off to the far side of the room, in the darkness, and I sat at the table by the lamp. The walls of that room were bright yellow, like a Vuillard, and the corners were in dark shadow. There was a very large mirror over the mantelpiece above the square table, it reflected the yellow light. Howard was standing aimlessly in the darkness, and Jo said, 'We've come to read your diaries.'

I wrote diaries then, every day before I went to sleep I wrote down everything that happened. And ever since I'd fallen in love with Howard I had written as the last words of each daily entry, 'I love Howard.' Or: 'I love you.' In retrospect it seems very adolescent, but then I was sixteen, or seventeen by then, which is adolescent, and maybe that's when you define yourself in those kinds of terms: I am the one who loves Howard. Howard is who I love. I love Howard. And of course the diaries contained multitudinous secrets, endless petty gripes and nastinesses, all the detritus of daily life, my ugly feelings, that ended up in this secret waste disposal unit, page after page covered in black scribble. And the notebooks: I kept a daily journal, or diary, a record of events, and in tandem I wrote in big black notebooks, I wrote the excess, what wouldn't fit, great splurges of emotion and analysis — what I would now call analysis. So I was pretty shocked when Jo said, 'We've come to read your diaries.'

To me the diaries, the notebooks, were by definition unreadable. They were my secret, my most precious object. No one could read them. Yet I don't remember even hesitating. I don't remember taking a minute to consider refusing them this request. Trying to be casual, in a gesture of complete abjection, I said, 'But of course!' I went to the place where I kept the books, and I said, 'Which ones do you want?'

Jo said, 'This year, and last year. And the notebooks.'

And I handed them over.

The two of them sat down at the table, and it was my turn to stand around the room aimlessly. Sidelong, I watched them turn the pages. I remember sensing a certain embarrassment on Howard's part, as if he didn't really want to be doing this to me. But it was also like a scene in a Resistance movie, this extraordinary moment, when they divided the diaries between them. Jo took this year's, Howard took last year's, in order to find out my secrets. I thought, 'I've got nothing left to lose.' I think it must have been a shock to Howard to read those three words, 'I love Howard', ending each scrawled entry, since I'd never said it to him directly. I thought he wouldn't like it. I remember he started to read and then obviously sickened of this task, he resorted to merely leafing through, glancing at things as they struck his eye. Jo was more systematic; I think she was looking for stuff I'd written about her.

I'd been seeing her brother, Philip, we'd been dating, or something like that, in some crazed and complicated scenario of revenge and substitution. As I said at the time to Nina, our mutual friend, I said, 'Well obviously it goes without saying that the nearest I can get to fucking Jo is to fuck Philip.' Nina was a little shocked, I think. Also I have to admit that I'd always suspected that Jo wanted to sleep with her brother, and couldn't, whereas I could, and did. I liked Philip, but the situation was so over-determined it wasn't really possible for us to find or make a relation that was our own, to say the least, so we gave up on it pretty quickly. Also I'd come off the pill, another gesture of abnegation, as if renouncing my claims on Howard meant giving up sex altogether. We tended to be slightly puritanical in those days about the pill; we thought you should start taking it when you entered into a serious relationship, that somehow being on it all the time was a sign of being a bit too loose, or easygoing. And we were terribly *sérieuse*.

In any case I never got any contraceptives together when I was seeing Philip, so we'd have these slightly contorted sexual encounters, and though he was very beautiful and very lovely — he had lovely long eyes and very soft skin, just like Jo's — it really didn't work. Anyway, when Jo was reading my diary she finally found something to point to, she pointed her finger to the words: 'Philip says Jo is a tough cookie.' I remember the

Generosity

other thing Philip said was, 'I don't know how people like Howard can exist.' I think she was a little disappointed.

My suspicion was that she wanted to prove something to Howard, and that was hard for me to imagine. I mean at the time I didn't picture them spending their time talking about me and what I felt and what I meant to them, but of course that's what they did. I was much more important to them than I ever let myself imagine. And then of course I'd confided in Jo, I'd told her (almost) everything (I didn't talk about sex with her, but then I didn't talk about sex with anyone at all then), most of all I'd told her over and over again how passionate I was about Howard, and how beautiful I found him and on and on and on. The things I felt I was forbidden to say to him. And she must have been trying to get Howard to see this, because he'd refused to — I'd kept this overwhelming passion carefully hidden from him, knowing it would scare him to death. He was skittish enough anyway, and he seemed to want me to be very cool, and I wanted to be what he wanted me to be, so I was very cool, very undemanding, very detached. I never said I love you, I never said, your beautiful eyes, your lovely neck, your pale skin. I never said those things. And he never said them to me.

So I think that the whole project of 'reading the diaries' was to demonstrate to Howard the extreme discrepancies between my silence and my emotion. To make it clear to him that I was madly in love, and thus to shift his perception of me, to make him want to get away from me, even. That's what I suspected, later, anyway. And I colluded with Jo in this, in some way I invited their invasion, and I think it was insane that I let them do it. Because no one had ever read my notebooks and diaries before, and it turned out that I could write them only if I was certain of their inviolability. This act of reading demolished that once and for all. Empty-handed, I stopped writing altogether.

What I do remember is that after Jo left for the States (which wasn't very long afterwards) Howard asked me round to his house, his parents' house, and he took me up to his little room

99

and sat me down at the desk with its white formica top where once I wrote a line in pencil, a backhanded declaration of love, he took me up to this room where we'd spent so much time and taken drugs and where he'd fucked me for the first time, where I'd lost my virginity, that is, and he opened one of the drawers in the desk and brought out a few sheets of paper and he said, 'I wanted to give you these, to make it equal, because I've read your stuff now, so you can read this.' And then he looked at one of them, and said, 'Oh no, not this one!' and laughed, and he put that one back in the drawer, and then he said, 'I'll go out for a while, now,' and he left me with two or three poems he'd written about me when we were going out together. And they were very beautiful, and I wished I'd known about them before.

And then, of course, I opened the drawer and I read the one that I wasn't supposed to read, which was a poem that compared me and Jo, unfavourably. He described my miserable face, puffy with depression and flu, and then the thrill and pleasure of seeing her, surrounded by colours, in the artists' materials shop where she was working. Needless to say this poem managed to undo any pleasure I might have had in the love poems he'd given me to read. I remember it ended with an expression of disgust, 'ugh!' he wrote, and I was devastated. Later I told Nina about it, and she said she thought the 'ugh!' was quite funny, it was so desperate and so extreme. But when your lover writes 'ugh!' about you when you're seventeen it isn't very funny really. Now it's kind of a scream, sort of.

Kwakiutl coppers were useless and very beautiful objects, not unlike a shield, made of rolled and beaten copper. In Kwakiutl culture during the nineteenth and early twentieth centuries, the copper was the most precious thing one could possess.

Coppers are vaguely oblong in shape, usually about eighteen inches long, curving at the apex, with sides narrowing at an angle from the top to the middle part, and then diverging slightly or staying parallel below. The upper portion is often engraved with the image of a face, while the lower rectangle has only two perpendicular ridges, making a T-shape across the lower half. It is a complex shape, which Lévi-Strauss describes as 'enigmatic'. The copper from which these objects were made may have originally come from Indian bands in Alaska, but by 1800 it was intermittently available through trading with the Europeans, who carried sheets of it to repair leaks in their ships. According to Marcel Mauss, the mythological sequence goes: springtime, arrival of salmon, new sun, red colour, copper.

Each copper had a name, for example: Sea Lion, Killer Whale, Noisy Copper, Quarrel Maker, Moon, All Other Coppers are Ashamed to Look at It. Thus the coppers are 'like' a man (with a face and a name, and a body traced in the T-shape), like salmon, like the sun after the winter ice, like life. Coppers were useful solely as representations of wealth; they could be bought and sold, cut up into pieces, broken in the fire, or, most dramatically, thrown into the sea.

Coppers were central to the culture of the potlatch. In order to humiliate the other, one is generous to him. To shame him, one showers him with objects, one 'buys' his copper. The copper then represents the excessive liberality of the chief who thus acquired it; a copper's value is measured by rivalry. To reduce the other to a state of abjection, one destroys objects of value, coppers, throwing them away.

Mauss records, quoting Boas, that in 1910, the copper Lesaxalayo was worth 9,000 woollen blankets (each worth about $4), 50 canoes, 6,000 button blankets (red and blue flannel blankets with mass-produced mother-of-pearl buttons sewn all over them in elaborate patterns), 260 silver bracelets, 60 gold bracelets, 70 gold earrings, 40 sewing machines, 25 gramophones, and 50 masks.

George Hunt recounts the true story of two Kwakiutl chiefs, who were great friends, called Fastrunner and Throwaway. Throwaway invited the clan of his friend to a feast of salmon berries, but he carelessly served the oil and berries in dishes that weren't perfectly clean. Fastrunner was offended; he refused the food, and lay down with his black bear blanket drawn over his face. All his relatives, seeing these signs of his displeasure, followed his example. Whereupon Throwaway urged them to eat, and the ceremonial speaker replied: 'Our chief will not eat the dirty things you have offered, O dirty man.' Throwaway was offended in his turn, and said: 'You speak as if you were a person of very great wealth.' This was equivalent to throwing down the gauntlet. Fastrunner replied: 'Indeed I am,' and sent his runners to bring his copper, Sea Monster. Fastrunner pushed the copper into the fire, in order 'to put out the fire of his rival'. This gesture of destruction must be matched, and Throwaway sent for his copper, called Looked at Askance, and he too pushed it into the fire, 'to keep it burning.' But Fastrunner had another copper, Crane, and he sent for that and placed it upon the fire, 'to smother it.' Throwaway was thus defeated, having no other copper to destroy.

However the next day, to carry this scene of rivalry and humiliation to its conclusion, Fastrunner returned the feast, and sent his attendants to invite Throwaway and all his relatives. In the night, Throwaway had feverishly pledged enough property to borrow another copper. So when the feast began, he refused to eat (using the same words which Fastrunner had used the day before) and sent his runners to bring the copper Day Face. He laid this on the fire, and extinguished it. Fastrunner rose and spoke: 'Now is my fire extinguished. Wait; sit down and see the deed that I shall do.' He 'put on the excitement' of the Dance of Fools (the secret society of which he was a member) and he sent for four canoes, belonging to his father-in-law. These canoes were heaped on the fire in the feasting-house, to take away the shame of having their fire extinguished. The flames were terrifying, fuelled by lashings of oolachan fish grease, yet Fastrunner's guests had to remain sitting there, or admit defeat. The black bear blanket of Throwaway was scorched, and under the blanket the skin of his legs blistered, but he sat tight. When the blaze diminished, he arose as if nothing had happened, and took some food as if to demonstrate his complete indifference to the extravagance of his rival.

These gestures of waste, sacrifice, and rivalry escalated between the two chiefs, until finally Fastrunner killed a slave. The body of the slave was cut up by the Fool Dancers and the Grizzly Bear Society, and then apparently eaten by the Hamatsa. The scalp he gave to Throwaway, who could not match this mighty deed. Later Throwaway and his warriors set forth on a warlike expedition against another band, and none of them returned. As Ruth Benedict writes: 'The characteristic Kwakiutl response to frustration was sulking and acts of desperation.'

One day Carrie came home from school and found signs that someone, some foreign body, had been in the flat. Tina was in Italy at the time, staying with their mother. They always left the front window unlocked, in case someone was late or forgot their keys; it was very easy to clamber over the sill. First she found a teapot, cold tea, and a dirty cup in the sink. Then she went to the loo; sitting on the toilet she looked and saw one long dark hair lying in the bottom of the bathtub. 'Someone has been here, drinking tea,' she thought. 'Whoever it was took a bath.' Walking into the front room, Carrie noticed a note beside the phone, with some coins on it. It read: 'Debbie rang. Here's some money for some calls I made to Oxford.' It was Howard, of course, Carrie recognized the writing. Her heart was beating fast now, she felt violated and at the same time very sorry she'd missed him. In a kind of emotional reflex, she took her notebook, and sat down to write. Opening the page, she saw his writing again. She felt her neck blush, reddening, as her eyes flew across the words, taking it in.

SONG
I I I I I me me me me meee
I I I I I me me me me meee
Me mine me mine me mine me mine I I I self

Me I me mine me I me mine my my my my self
meself myself meself myself mine I mine I mee
I I I I I mee me mee me mee
          BY MYSELF

Terrified, she immediately leafed through the whole notebook, scanning quickly, panicking, to see what Howard might
have read. Then the anger rose thick in her throat, and she
looked up. There was a picture on her wall, a small reproduction
of a painting called *Crime Passionel*; it showed a woman shooting
a man. Yellow fire burst out of the gun, red blood dripped
from his brow onto the floor. For one moment, Carrie wanted
a gun. She felt like killing somebody.

She read: *The theme of honour through ruin is fundamental to
North-West American potlatch.* Honour through ruin, it could
be emblazoned on her shield: an empty cornucopia, perhaps,
dripping blood? Melodrama, again, always the resort to melodrama — if you exaggerate, theatricalize, you can see the
absurdity, protect yourself. Carrie was amused to think of her
path through life as one great potlatch, or one potlatch after
another. Honour through ruin. She read about the Kwakiutl,
working through the long winter, how they would carve boxes
and canoes, and pile up Hudson's Bay Company blankets, five
pairs to a box, and save up the oolachan fish grease, all their
luxuries, and then on very specific special occasions, the head
of a family or a kinship group would hold a potlatch, and invite
everyone, and give it all away.

The more you could give away, the more powerful you were.
The Kwakiutl were obsessed with status: every person of
rank had three or four names, linking them to various kinship
groups and secret societies, within which they took up carefully
differentiated positions in relation to those above and below
them in rank. The system was so elaborate that no one was
quite equal to anyone else. Each time such a position was taken

up, a name and its associated privileges was claimed, a potlatch had to be given. The guests in effect approved the claim, by witnessing the ritual dances, taking part in the feasts, and by accepting gifts suitable to each guest's rank and position. The tally-keeper memorized precisely who received what, as if to preclude later controversy.

Apart from claiming your name and position, the other occasion on which a potlatch could occur, the other great function of potlatches, was in order to wipe out shame.

Of course the Anglos couldn't make it out at all, and predictably, the government tried their best to suppress the practice of potlatch. Meanwhile the Indians continued to hold secret, underground potlatches. At one point in the 1920s, it was planned that the ceremonial dances would take place before a public audience in the local community centre, like the YMCA, under the guise of a demonstration or exhibition of folk-dancing, and then later in the evening, under cover of darkness, the host and his tally-keeper (who these days was allowed to write everything down instead of memorizing it) would go from house to house, ringing the doorbells, and handing out appropriate gifts in the form of cash. Such were the lengths to which the Kwakiutl were willing to go in order to perpetuate the celebration of potlatch.

The other great ritual that the Europeans objected to was the Hamatsa dances, the Hamatsa being the highest and most prestigious of the ceremonial secret societies. The dancers personified a terrible bird-monster who fed on human flesh, and the most thrilling part of the dance was when the Hamatsa, in a state of ecstasy, took great bites out of various members of the audience. European observers were horrified by this bloody spectacle, especially when the dancer would then spit out a great chunk of raw flesh, to the delight of the audience. It transpired later that this apparent cannibalism was a very secret, carefully planned special effect, involving planted stooges (who were rewarded for being cut or bit), as well as effigies, dead animals, sleight of hand, bladders of blood, etc. This sophisticated combination of elaborate stage manipulation, sado-masochistic display, and extreme frenzy was incomprehensible to the empire builders, who banned the Hamatsa dancers also.

The Kwakiutl were always enthusiastic traders with the Europeans, exchanging furs for Hudson's Bay Company blankets (mass-produced in the mills of Yorkshire), and copper sheeting, to make coppers, and steel tools with which they developed the already very advanced art of carving masks and boxes and canoes and totem poles. Eventually, at the potlatch, they were giving away sewing machines, and willow-pattern china, and crates of oranges, bought with their earnings in the fish-canneries and the brothels.

The smallpox epidemics of the 1860s wiped out one-third of the Indian population of British Columbia. One outcome of this decimation was a dramatic breakdown in the elaborate system of rank and status, simply because there weren't enough people left to fill all the positions. Rampant and wildcat potlatches followed, in which more and more ostentatious displays of reckless expenditure took place. A late version of potlatch pushed this excessive expenditure further, towards sheer waste, where instead of giving all this stuff away, it would simply be destroyed. They would build a shelter like a barn, and heap up all the blankets and boxes and canoes and fish grease and sewing machines, and then set fire to it.

When William Duncan set up Metlakatla, these things were forbidden: 'The Demoniacal Rites called Medicine Work; Conjuring and all the heathen practices over the sick; Use of intoxicating liquor; Gambling; Painting Faces; Giving away property for display; tearing up property in anger or to wipe out disgrace.'

Carrie stopped. Waste, sacrifice, rivalry, gift: in the logic of potlatch, the most powerful one is the one who remains empty-handed.

Dysplasia

For Nature has placed inside women's bodies in a secret intestinal place an animal, a member, which is not in man, in which sometimes are engendered certain saline, nitrous, boracic, acrid, biting, shooting, bitterly tickling humors, through whose prickling and grievous wriggling (for this member is very nervous and sensitive) the entire body is shaken, all the senses ravished, all inclinations unleashed, all thoughts confounded . . .

François Rabelais, *The Heroic Deeds and Sayings of the Good Pantagruel,* Book III, chapter xxxii (1584)

The Photographer . . . needs in many cases no aid from any language of his own, but prefers rather to listen, with the picture before him, to the silent but telling language of nature — It is unnecessary for him to use the vague terms which denote a difference in the degree of mental suffering, as for instance, distress, sorrow, deep sorrow, grief, melancholy, anguish, despair; the picture speaks for itself with the most marked pression and indicates the exact point which has been reached in the scale of unhappiness between the first sensation and its utmost height . . .

Hugh W. Diamond, *On the Application of Photography to the Physiognomic and Mental Phenomena of Insanity* Read before the Royal Society, 22 May 1856 *a malady through representation*

It was always unclear whether there was something wrong with her, or not.

The woman said the cervix looked lacerated. She asked Gina if she had had an abortion. Gina hadn't, then. The woman said, because your cervix looks lacerated. Then she said, deformed.

So it was never very clear whether there was something wrong with her, or not. Something looked wrong, clearly. That woman had called in another doctor, an older woman, who took one look (Gina lying flat, the speculum inserted) and said, D-E-S. It was the first time Gina'd heard of it. Gina was nineteen.

She wrote a letter to her mother in Paris, and her mother wrote back. Yes, she'd taken it, she said she'd taken it, this drug, diethylstilboestrol, she'd taken it throughout her pregnancy with Gina. The drug was meant to prevent miscarriage; that's why her mother took it. The doctors stopped prescribing it to pregnant women some time in the 1960s. It was known to cause malformations of the cervix and vagina; it was known to cause cancer; no one knew what else it did. Thus Gina found herself one of a group, a group of daughters, women who apparently had something wrong with them, maybe.

No other doctor, and there were many of them over the years, peering up into her inner recesses, her nether cavities, her cunt, no other doctor ever exclaimed at the sight of her cervix quite like that. Sometimes Gina wondered if the woman had been exaggerating. Was it simply that the other doctors were more guarded, or tactful? Better trained to deal with this monstrosity? Lacerated. Deformed. Or maybe they didn't notice, maybe there was really nothing to see.

Gina looked it up in the dictionary. The chemical formula was asymmetric, like her cervix: $OHC_6H_4CH:CHC_6H_4OH$.

There was nothing (seriously) wrong with her. There was nothing wrong with her.

hysterosalpingogram

What do I remember? It's so hard to say. I remember this doctor in Chicago, this woman doctor, saying to me, 'Well, I'm sorry to have to tell you this, but with your history, you will have grave fertility problems.'

I liked her, this woman doctor, but I found it exhausting: having to take all these drugs, all this fucking metronidazole, and doxycycline, and at the same time, having to take in the idea of 'grave fertility problems' as some kind of inevitability. My very own scarred Fallopian tubes.

And then there's the cancer stuff. I have to have these regular special cancer tests or investigations, scrutinies really, they scrutinize my interior, the doctors, anyway I have to have them at regular intervals because my mother took this drug when she was pregnant with me. It seeped through her placenta, like poison. It was meant to prevent miscarriage, and as she always says, I was the most wanted baby in the world. Most wanted, like a criminal, I always think. Anyway, the drug makes me susceptible to a form of cancer that never existed before, a form of cancer that apparently is only found in the female children of women who took diethylstilboestrol during pregnancy. The threatened cancer is cancer of the vagina, which is relatively dire, because when it happens they have to more or less take your vagina out. You become like a sex change person, someone with a little hollow instead of a vagina, a little concavity to signify the possibility of penetration, or femininity, or something.

I suppose by that time you're glad you're still alive. Apparently this horror show is not very likely to happen to me though, because it seems to take place before you're twenty, if it's going to happen at all. On the other hand, we're all under fifty, us DES daughters, so they really don't know what's going to happen to us as we get older. That's the reason to keep an eye on us, give us regular colposcopies.

A colposcopy is like this: you lie on your back on a table with your legs drawn up, like an ordinary exam, but the table rises up hydraulically, so that the doctor sitting comfortably at the end of the table is looking directly into your vagina. Your cunt is at his eye level, in other words. He inserts a speculum, and then a kind of microscope, so that the cells of the vaginal wall are seen in extreme close up. Usually there is a big black Nikormat camera attached to the colposcope, in case they see anything worth photographing, and the doctor sits down and looks into you through two eye-pieces, just like binoculars. There is a third eye-piece, like a long thin telescope, that comes out of the top of the colposcope apparatus, allowing a third person to stand next to the seated doctor and peer into the inner recesses also. It's quite amusing, reminiscent of Jules Verne somehow, submarines.

Then he takes a bit of cotton wool and dips it in vinegar, and paints that on the walls of the vagina, all the while expressing doubt that you are in fact a DES baby. He looks at the effects of the vinegar and becomes even more vehement. 'There is no sign of any abnormality,' he says. I go on lying there, having been through this movie before. Whereupon he does the second test, which is to paint the vagina with iodine. Suddenly there's great excitement: a result. He says, 'Well, well, well,' very quickly, and calls his colleague over, who rushes up to peer into the telescope, as the first doctor frantically describes what they're both seeing. It's all Greek to me. The doctor looks up over my belly and says, 'This is textbook stuff, very good, we must get it on video next time!' He's thrilled. I'm pleased when, having accepted that I am indeed one of these DES cases, they have a good look at my weird cells and decide I don't have cancer, for the time being. I'm allowed to get dressed, to go home.

In the office, the doctor rubs his hands together and says, 'Right! We'll see you again in what — six months? That's a bit soon, isn't it? Let's say nine months — six is too short, twelve is too long! Let's say nine!' I say, all right.

Thus every nine months, instead of giving birth to a baby, I go and have my cancer test. It's always a bit nerve-wracking; I'm terrified they'll tell me I've got cancer, needless to say. But they are very nice to me, and quite often they invite visitors, spectators, so to speak, to look at my special effects, to see how the vinegar does nothing, but one mustn't be downcast, because the iodine performs like fireworks in there. Watch.

The last time, last year, I saw this very nice woman who had previously been the sort of second in command, the one standing over the spyglass, peering in with one eye screwed shut. She seemed to be Italian, originally, and she did the whole vinegar and iodine routine, during which I'm lying there, fingers crossed, and then she said, 'I don't like what I see.' I went into shock. Then she said, 'But I think you should come back and see the consultant. I'm really a fertility specialist, not a cancer specialist, and I can't really tell what I'm looking at.' I was surprised and really very pleased: most doctors don't let on when they don't know what they're doing. As I got dressed I told her some of my fertility anxieties: how this doctor in Chicago had said that my tubes were maybe blocked, how I'd had this infection and that disease, and I was worried because I wanted to have a baby, sometime. She said, 'I can refer you to my fertility clinic, here's the number, give us a call and make an appointment.' I was pleased, despite the cancer stuff.

So I had to come back and see the Great Man Himself. His name was Dr Savage, if you can believe it. But he was terribly busy, or something, so I had to wait a couple of weeks before I could see him. I was quite scared. When I finally went for my appointment, I almost went to the wrong hospital. I quite often make slips like that with my cancer tests, I go to Gower

Street instead of Goodge Street, and then I have to run, not to be late. Anyway, there were hordes of spectators this time, like five people (mostly men) in this little room, and most surprisingly of all, right beside me as I reclined on the examination table, was a massive, 24–inch Sony Trinitron video monitor, which seemed to be attached to a little video camera that was going to be aimed into my vagina.

The TV set was about three inches away from me, conveniently angled so that the doctor performing the colposcopy could see the magnified image on the TV screen, rather than having to look through the binoculars. I was quite excited: I'd never seen my cervix on TV before. When it appeared on the screen, I was completely surprised. It didn't look the way I expected it to at all. The colours were truly lurid: livid greys, and shiny shell-like pinks, and dark purples. The wall of the vagina was like a dark cave, purple-grey ridges reminiscent of a cathedral cut in stone, shadowy and even somehow threatening. And the cervix itself, pale pink and wet and shining: it was terribly poetic. Everything was magnified, so that the cervix virtually filled the enormous glowing screen. It was monstrous, a sci-fi nightmare, but at the same time the cervix was sort of breathtaking, if a bit lopsided and irregular, one of the effects of the DES.

I remember being amazed that all the people in the room were talking about my vagina while looking at the TV screen. I mean, I was used to them peering into me, and discussing what they saw, but now people could actually point at the TV screen, completely separate from me. They'd say, 'What about that bit?' in a kind of speculative tone, touching the TV screen with a finger, and then a gigantic wooden stick with a little wad of cotton wool on the end would suddenly appear, and sort of poke or prod the bit of my vagina or cervix pointed to, to see how it would respond. It seemed an extraordinary combination of extremely primitive behaviour (like a kid poking rotten leaves or mud with a stick he's found) with a kind of ultimate scientific hi-tech: the video image, in living

colour, of my interior. I saw them apply the vinegar, and then
the iodine, and I could even begin to make out what all the
fuss was about, how the oddball cells didn't 'take up' the iodine
the way you'd imagine they would. I began to feel a bit sorry for
my cervix, exposed to all these eyes, this seemingly somewhat
unscientific prodding. The light they shine up there is very
bright and hot, like a spotlight; my cervix was like a reluctant
star, caught in its flagrant glare.

The doctors seemed to be enjoying themselves, talking and
gesticulating, when finally, the great man, the man in control
of the camera, Doc Savage, this man put his hand gently on
my inner thigh, he looked up from my cunt, and he said, 'Let's
do a biopsy! Why not?'

Someone said, 'I wouldn't watch this bit if I were you.' Still,
it was hard not to look. They take this extraordinary instrument
like tongs, or scissors really, more like very long, thin scissors,
with a little scoop on the end, and they cut a little piece of
flesh out of your cervix. I saw the lump of red stuff on the end
of the scissors when he pulled it out. Then they seal the wound
they've made with silver nitrate; it reminded me somehow of
the sulphur melting on the head of a match. I watched that
bit. There's some bleeding. And then the doctors trooped out,
and I was told to get dressed. It would take two weeks for the
results of the biopsy to come through.

So I waited. Eventually I telephoned on the day I was told
I could, and the head nurse said, 'We are writing to you.'
And I knew that it must be OK, otherwise they wouldn't write.
So it was all over, until next time. And I was very happy,
though quite exhausted emotionally by it all.

Then I called the nice Italian fertility doctor, and made an
appointment with her. I thought, I'm going to get all this over
with at once. I made the appointment, and I went to see her,
I was practising my speech, my explanation, my request, and
when I got into her office, out it all came. She told me I could
have what's called an HSG, which is where they take an X-ray
photo of your Fallopian tubes, to see if they're blocked or not.

She said it would be interesting to see if the tubes had been affected by the DES, as well. I'd never thought of that.

When the day came I was very frightened, because I knew it was going to be painful, but also I was scared about what I would find out. As I was leaving I said to Patrick, 'This is what you might call elective torture.' I couldn't remember why I'd ever wanted to do this thing, but he reminded me, he said, 'You decided that if you had to have a terrible trauma about infertility, you might as well have it now.' It sort of made sense, vaguely.

I went to the hospital, and found the X-ray department with some difficulty. It was quite hilarious on one level, because everyone in the room — an enormous room, full of massive pieces of equipment — everyone was wearing lead aprons. I thought, where's *my* lead apron? As I lay down under this gigantic X-ray apparatus, I joked with the nurse, I said, 'I guess you don't have to work out at the gym if you wear one of those all day.' At first she didn't know what I was talking about, then she laughed. They were all pretty skinny.

The X-ray doctor was a young man, and he said, 'Why are we doing this?' I was slightly taken aback. I explained. Then I asked him what HSG stands for. He said, 'Hysterosalpingogram.' Then I said, 'This is like putting in an IUD, right?' and he said, 'Yes exactly, that's exactly what it's like.' Then he described the procedure. You lie down on an enormous table, with this massive machine hanging from the very high ceiling looming over you, very Frankenstein, and the doctor puts a speculum up you, and then he dilates the cervix (ow!) and inserts a catheter into it, and then he lines up the X-ray apparatus and squirts iodine (which is resistant to X-rays) into the uterus. The iodine fills the uterus, and then it runs down the Fallopian tubes, and spills out the ends where they form these sort of trumpet-like cones to catch the egg as it bursts out of the ovary. That's if they're unblocked. Otherwise, the iodine fills the tube to the point of scarring or blockage, and you can see where that point is. It's relatively straightforward. Then he takes the picture.

What was stunning, though, was the fact that again there was a little video monitor beside the examination table. The doctor uses the video image to line up the X-ray still camera, in order to get the best possible shot. He asked me if I wanted to watch, and I said, 'Of course.' This time the video image was like something out of 1940s science fiction, Buck Rogers maybe: it was black and white, and the image itself was oval, a kind of horizontal ellipse, framed within the black rectangle of the TV screen. And since of course X-rays aren't good for you (cf. lead aprons everywhere), the doctor would so to speak throw the X-ray on, in a kind of blast of light, and this very degraded, fuzzy black and white oval image of my pelvis would appear, momentarily, on the little TV screen, and then fade again, like a light going out. Again, it was terribly poetic.

I was tremendously uncomfortable, because I had all this equipment crammed in my vagina, and instead of being allowed to have my legs drawn up, like a frog, I had to lie them down flat, which was very difficult and very uncomfortable. I mean, it was painful, but you call it discomfort in that context, in the context of elective torture. So I had all this gear inside of me, this syringe of iodine and catheter and speculum, and my legs stretched out straight, and the doctor dressed in lead, adjusting everything with the help of brief bursts of X-ray video imaging. I could see the thigh bones fitting into the pelvis, and the metal instruments in my vagina. When he had everything lined up in the right position, he shot the iodine into my uterus. We both watched the oval TV image. It was extraordinary: the little triangular uterus took form as the iodine filled it — the iodine appearing as flat white on this fuzzy TV screen — and then suddenly, momentarily, these two very fine lines were drawn, emerging from the points of the triangle, very fine lines meandering wildly like an ancient river delta. I'd always imagined the Fallopian tubes were like a sort of straight line, a tube from the ovary to the uterus, but they're not; they're very long, and very thin, and the iodine outlined their multiple curving zigzags until it reached the point where it spilled, a blurry fountain, out of the ends.

That meant the tubes were OK. I was elated. The two fine meandering lines were drawn so quickly, instantaneously, it was like magic, and I watched it all, elated, in such painful discomfort and yet so elated, and at the same time thinking, how unbearable this would be if the tubes were blocked, and you saw it all, live on TV. It was like a shadow, the possibility of what it might have been like. As it was, I felt fantastic. The doctor took a couple of still X-rays of the configuration of uterus and tubes, and then slowly removed the instruments from my vagina.

I felt the opposite of what I've felt all these years, damaged; I felt like my dear old tubes had been under attack from all these drugs and diseases, and they'd survived somehow, they'd fended off the invasion, preserved themselves against the minuscule hordes of microbes and bacteria and poison. (I always love that bit in *Notorious* when she says, 'They're poisoning me.') And there was something so perverse about figuring myself as feminine — as maternal, potentially — through the mediation of this elaborate medical technology, this technical imagining. A strange kind of reparation, some kind of return to the mother's body, via the fascinations of the video screen.

I'd pictured my mother's body, surging with artificial hormones, prescribed to her by idiots; my beloved mother who says to me, 'I took it every single day, from the third day of pregnancy to the moment you were born!' I'd pictured my own body: blocked, scarred, damaged. Now there was another image, almost unbelievable, narrow rivers meandering through the delta of my belly. The ghastly joke, the absurd literalization of the feminine metaphor that was my body, moved over, it shifted somehow. I didn't have to obsess about it any more, about the baby I wouldn't have; I could forget about it, now.

dilation

To Gina, the word daughter always sounded like it contained the word ought, the sound you make when gagging or retching. As a child, there were a number of different foods, like tapioca pudding, for example, which caused Gina to gag, or retch. Much later some of her worst nightmares contained an overwhelming, amorphous white mass, or shape, like an endless heap of shaving cream but more substantial, gelatinous, both fluid and solid, an image of absolute viscosity. She wondered if this were the tapioca pudding, come back to haunt her. Or perhaps, more ominously, her mother's gigantic white breast, an indelible memory of those first few weeks, of gagging, swallowing, and retching.

When Gina read that newborn babies always lose weight in the first ten days after birth, that the struggle with the mother for food invariably entails a certain element of difficulty, not to say starvation, she was profoundly comforted. So Freud was right, after all, she thought, there's no such thing as the perfect mother.

When Gina was fifteen, virginal, her mother said to her, in her mother's bedroom she suddenly turned to her, she spoke with vehemence, she said, 'You girls are so romantic about sex. Losing your virginity is awful, you really shouldn't have high expectations, it's hell. It hurts like hell, there's blood everywhere, you wake up in the morning all sticky, your legs all covered with —' at this point her mother hesitated momentarily, a conceptual hiccup in her tirade '— with the shoot-out from his penis,' she continued. 'It's *awful.*'

Gina thought, I think I'd rather maintain my romantic illusions than replace them with this insistent image of physical disgustingness. She tried to think of sticky thighs with some kind of enthusiasm. It was hard to imagine liking it.

Somehow, at this time, in her imagination, the sexual exchange of bodily fluids seemed bearable if they stayed in the appropriate place. The semen was meant to be in the vagina, not all over your legs. She couldn't do anything with it, this image too vivid and shocking to forget or efface.

Later Gina thought, why couldn't she just say 'come'. You wake up in the morning covered in come. Still, then, she probably would have found that an equally revolting idea, or word.

Later still Gina wondered at her mother's representation of sex. For years she'd interpreted pronouncements such as these to mean her mother didn't like it. Then she thought that was probably all wrong. (It was amazing how many people believed their parents didn't like it. As if the idea of them liking it were more than they could bear.) But her mother wanted to warn them, to protect her daughters, in case *they* didn't like it. Like it really wasn't very nice, and they ought to know.

When Gina was sixteen and three quarters, her mother and her older sister Amy were sitting in the kitchen, talking about losing your virginity. It was a hot topic in those days. Gina was standing at the sink, she was making coffee; her mother and sister carried on talking as if she wasn't there. They were talking about what the best age was, the best age to lose your virginity. Amy'd first done it at fifteen; that seemed a bit young. Finally they agreed sixteen was best.

Standing there, Gina smiled awkwardly, terribly shy, and said, 'I guess I haven't got much time.'

They both turned surprised faces up to her, and almost simultaneously, her mother and older sister cried, 'Oh *you'll* never lose *your* virginity, Gina!' Whereupon all three women fell about laughing.

When Gina was eleven she was sitting in the living-room while her mother and a wonderfully glamorous girlfriend of her mother's drank coffee and smoked cigarettes and talked. She was very struck by a joke her mother's friend told, because she didn't understand it.

Three women are in the front seat of a convertible, driving down to a party in the country. One of them puts her hand out, in front of her face, and she says, I have such small hands, it's difficult to find gloves small enough and fine enough to fit them, they are so lovely and small. The second lifts up one of her feet and contemplates it, saying, I have the tiniest feet of anyone I know, they are so little and perfect. They go on and on like this for a while, showing off their tiny hands and little feet, until the third woman gets annoyed. Finally she says, has anyone got a Band-Aid? I think I've got the curse.

There was another joke, from that time, that Gina found equally perplexing. This one she read in a letter from her best friend, Zoë, who was out of town during the summer:

> Why did Cinderella scream in the night?
> Because her tampax turned into a pumpkin.

Another time, Gina heard her mother say, again to this very sophisticated, glamorous friend, she said, 'When my daughters are fifteen I'll just take them straight to the gynaecologist and have them fitted with IUDs. I mean, what else is one supposed to do?' It was 1967.

In the event, as her daughters got older, Gina's mother offered no contraceptive advice whatever. This was consonant with her previous practice in sex education.

When Gina was six, and her sister eight, her mother sat them down one summer afternoon, while Daddy was taking a nap. She said, 'I suppose you know by now how a man makes love to a woman?'

Both girls nodded solemnly. Amy said, '*You* don't know.'

Gina said, 'Yes, I do, you told me.'

Amy said, 'No I didn't.'

'Yes you did,' Gina said.

'I never told you,' Amy said. 'You don't know anything.'

'Yes you did,' Gina said.

Only a few weeks before, Amy had forced this information on Gina, who felt no curiosity about it, if anything, a certain resistance to it. She knew she wouldn't like it, whatever it was.

Amy said, 'Do you know how babies are made?'

Gina said, 'They come out of your stomach.'

Gina always imagined hospital doctors in white masks cutting you open, a huge gash across your tummy, to let the baby out. She was very anxious thinking about cavemen, though, because she knew they didn't have sharp knives then, or hospitals, or anything. She thought all the women in those times must have died when they had a baby, their stomachs bursting when the baby got too big. Then she thought, that can't be right. She thought they must have used sharpened flints, and sewed up the wound with sinew. It seemed both terrifyingly dangerous and somewhat unlikely. But how else could you get the baby *out*?

In any case, this vision of reproductive violence may have been one reason she was reluctant to hear what Amy had to say.

It was a similar problem to the question of the radio top ten, a question that plagued her a couple of years later. She didn't know how they decided a particular record would be number one. She came to the conclusion that all radios were secretly two-way radios, and the people from the radio station listened in, to hear what people were saying about the different records. She started talking to her clock-radio, mimicking realistic conversations, in which two or more voices discussed the Dave Clark Five versus the Zombies, in an attempt to get her favourite record into the top ten. After a couple of days of this, she gave up. It seemed too unlikely, simply. In Gina's world, apparently, there was no one she could ask about these things.

Amy said, 'No I mean how babies are made. What you have to *do*.'

Gina didn't know. She didn't want to know. She thought you got married and then the babies came along. She said nothing. Amy tormented her: 'Don't you want to know? Don't you want me to tell you?'

Finally Amy said, 'The man spits in your po-po.' (Po-po was the term the family used for vagina.)

Gina tried to pretend she wasn't shocked.

Gina's mother interrupted the two girls squabbling over who knew what. She may have been relieved that they were so certain she had nothing to tell them. She said, 'Well.' They looked up. 'Well,' she said again, 'no doubt you think it's disgusting —'

At this the two children solemnly nodded again.

'But,' her mother said with a smile, 'we think it's *funny!*'

Funny? It was unimaginable. That was it, that was all the sex education Gina got from either of her parents.

When she was nine, one afternoon, Gina went downstairs to her mother's room and complained of a stomach ache. She didn't really have a very bad stomach ache, but she thought she might be able to extract some sympathetic attention, and maybe even stay home from school the next day. Gina put her hand flat on her belly, below her navel, and standing in the doorway of her mother's enormous bedroom, whining slightly, she said, 'Mummy, I have a stomach ache.'

Her mother seemed bad-tempered, more than a little annoyed. She asked Gina what she'd eaten, how long she'd felt badly. Then her mother snapped, 'Oh God, maybe you're getting the curse.' She sounded as if this would be the last irritating straw.

Gina didn't know what that was, the curse. She told her mother she didn't know what that was. Her mother flipped.

'You don't *know*?!' she shrieked quietly. 'How can you not know? Don't the girls at school talk about it?'

Gina said no.

'Don't you have any friends who talk about it?'

Gina started to feel frightened, her mother seemed so angry. Her mother said, 'Surely they teach you about it, don't they? Doesn't the school teach you about it?'

Gina said no, she didn't know what her mother was talking about.

Her mother went on, 'Don't the other girls talk about it? Don't the older girls talk about it, on the bus?'

Gina tried to reconstruct overheard conversations on the bus home from school. Maybe she'd misunderstood, her mother seemed convinced that everyone was talking about this, but she didn't know what it was. 'No,' she said.

Her mother heaved an enormous sigh. She looked slightly panicked as she realized she would have to explain.

'When girls get to be eleven or twelve or so,' she said, 'they get the curse. That means that every month they bleed a little instead of peeing. I mean, blood comes out, instead of pee.'

'Oh,' Gina said, in a deadened voice. She really didn't like the sound of that; she pictured a thin stream of bright red blood pouring out of her into the toilet.

'And sometimes you get cramps, in your stomach, too,' her mother said, raising her eyebrows hopefully.

Gina's stomach ache vanished like a shadow. She felt exhausted; she said, 'I think I'll just go lie down for a minute.' Her mother turned back to the mirror, turning back to the task in hand.

In the end, Gina figured it out by a process of deduction, logically. Her friend Sally said the man's penis went into you. This seemed horrifyingly plausible. But there must be, Gina thought, remembering the spit, there must be something else. The man must leave something there, inside you, something from his body. Sally denied this, she was certain he just put it in and that was it, the mere act of penetration was enough, but Gina was convinced. After much thought, she decided the man must pee a little, inside of you. That was how babies were made.

A couple of years later Gina's friend Zoë loaned her a book her parents had given her. It was called *Everything a Young Girl*

Should Know about Sex. It didn't say anything about contraceptives, or sticky come on your legs in the morning, but it clarified some things a bit. Nevertheless, when Zoë suggested that perhaps you would have to spread your legs, doing it, so that the man could get at that bit of you, Gina wasn't sure. It was hard to imagine, doing it.

Then they read Edna O'Brien's novel *The Country Girls*, in which at one point the heroine describes fucking her husband, lying flat underneath him, with the soles of her feet gently rubbing the small of his back. Gina spent a long time trying to imagine the position they were in, for this conjunction of sole of foot and lower back to take place. Eventually she got the picture. Thus Zoë's hypothesis was confirmed; you did open your legs.

When Gina was twelve she got her period. She was on holiday in Sicily with her family, sharing a hotel room with her sister. (Later she thought it was probably very D. H. Lawrence to have her menarche in Taormina.) Gina was terrified her mother would find out, and flip. She knew she would turn it into the most amazing drama. Gina tried to keep her bleeding secret from everyone, thinking, if I can just manage till I get back to London, only a couple of days, then I can go to the chemist and buy some pads. She changed her underpants many times a day, as each new pair became soaked with blood. In the evening, she scrubbed her underpants in the bathroom sink, with the door locked, carefully arranging them as she hung them to dry on the towel rail so that the bloodstained part wouldn't show. Her sister Amy figured out what was happening almost immediately, but said nothing. Later Gina wondered at Amy's discretion; was it embarrassment, or the sheer intensity of Gina's denial? Perhaps Amy dreaded her mother's reaction as much as Gina did.

The night before they were leaving for London, Gina's mother was in the girls' bedroom, supervising the packing. Gina sensed how lucky she'd been, that she'd managed to keep the secret so far. As Gina leaned over a suitcase on the floor, suddenly her mother emitted a yelp of anguish; she'd spotted some blood on Gina's pyjamas. 'Oh my God,' she cried, 'you've got the curse!'

There ensued precisely the grand opera Gina feared, with shouting and uproar, puffing sighs of irritation, screeds of words aimed in any direction, at Gina's sister, her father, at Gina herself. When Amy wearily acknowledged the situation saying, 'I know, I know, it's been going on for a few days,' Gina realized for the first time that pathetically draping her bloodstained pants around the bathroom in elaborately deceptive folds hadn't succeeded in concealing anything. When her mother gave her half a box of kleenex to put in her underpants, Gina wanted to disappear.

a question of lay analysis

Gina was having dinner at home with her friend Patrick. They sat together at the table, drinking red wine and eating fruit.

'What was so comic about the photography angle, though,' she said, 'was that I could see it too. I'd sort of got used to being the object of scrutiny, the archetypal passive position, right? And then technology intervenes, and suddenly I could look — at myself. I could line up with the experts, at the same time as being laid out for them.'

'For their delectation,' Patrick gently insisted.

'Quite. But the structure is shifted, somehow, isn't it? When the cervix becomes *my* cervix, and I can see it too.'

'What I keep wondering is,' Patrick said, 'if there's never anything wrong with you, isn't there something rather exhibitionistic about all this?'

'Exhibitionistic? *Moi?!*' They laughed.

'I know what you mean,' Gina said. 'This perpetual display, compulsively going down to the hospital to spread my legs, so to speak. To show something off, something that until recently I myself had never seen, some invisible symptom . . .'

'Yes,' Patrick said.

'So according to you, I'm really the active one, clambering onto the examination table and inviting the speculum in? How vile.'

'Well, I think it may be a bit of both,' Patrick said, prudently.

'What, active and passive. Maybe. I tend to think there are two possible bodies here, the body that's damaged but not dying, and the body that's really irrevocably fucked up. The test tells me which one is mine; it repeatedly reconfirms what I already know, the conditions under which I live: that something's wrong, but it's all right, for the time being.'

Gina paused, peeling her peach with wet fingers. Then she went on. 'The way I see it, it's a triangulation situation, in which the relationship of mother and daughter is mediated by this discourse of authority, medicine. I think the doctors must stand in for Daddy in some weird way.'

'But isn't it also all tied with stuff about damaging the mother's body, à la Melanie Klein?' Patrick asked. 'I mean, doesn't Klein say the classic crisis for the daughter is that she's already torn the mother's body to pieces, biting, scratching, gouging, gnawing — you name it.'

'I always envisaged a sort of explosion,' Gina said, 'the baby really wanting to just blow the mother's body up.'

'Mmm.' Patrick paused momentarily. 'So how come you're so insistent that it was your mother who damaged you. I know Klein says little girls fear their mothers will —'

'*Eviscerate* them!' Gina shrieked.

'Precisely. So that turning the tables, reversing the terms, is part of a strategy of denial, maybe.'

'You mean,' Gina said, 'that I'm saying, again, I'm still saying, constantly, I'm saying: it's OK, I'm already damaged, and my mother is the one who did this to me, and I can bear it. Really, it's OK.'

'Yes,' Patrick said.

'So my accusation against her (*how could you do this to me?*) is actually a cover for my far more explosive and violent feelings, my fear of blowing her up.'

'Or a rationalization,' Patrick said. 'It's like, you won't submit to all that violence and passion, mother and daughter, daughter and mother. So you bring in a third term, you bring in the doctor and his, shall we say, *equipment*. You come up with another version — a version that's tolerable, barely, in which you're the one who's damaged, and you can cope, you can contain it, because she's the one who is in the wrong.'

Looking up, Gina spoke quickly. 'But what's so interesting is that in real life my actual mother doesn't seem to feel too bad about any of this stuff. She's terribly sane about it. First, she knows, she says, that there's nothing she can do about it. And then, she was only following doctor's orders, anyway; she was being the good little girl, or the good mother, gone awry. It's not her fault, in other words.'

'That clinches it, doesn't it?' Patrick said, smiling. 'Maybe if she'd responded differently to all this, if she'd shrieked and screamed, loud protestations of guilt and responsibility, maybe then you wouldn't have been able to use it as you have.'

'Which is?'

'Which is to be able to formulate an accusation against your mother, to accuse her of damaging you, irrevocably, without the fear of hurting her. She's well defended, she knows she was only trying to do the right thing.'

'I suspect she still thinks that if she hadn't taken all these precautions, she would have miscarried, and I wouldn't be here to complain about it. She didn't only take the drug, you know, she also spent a large part of the pregnancy in bed. Amy was two, or something, nearly two, and she just sat in the playpen watching TV, for months.'

'*Really?*' Patrick said.

'But recently when I thought I was pregnant, you remember, a couple of months ago, I talked to my mother on the phone, and she was telling me not to have too violent sex for a while, in case of causing a miscarriage, and I said, oh I have this theory of miscarriages, which is to let nature take its course, you know, maybe there's something wrong with the foetus, or whatever, and she roared with laughter and said, well if I'd thought that, you wouldn't be here now to have these theories!'

'So from her point of view, it really doesn't seem to be about her damaging you.'

'Absolutely not,' Gina said. 'From her point of view, it's another sign of love. But I have to hang on to this story, this tale of woe. I give her the power to harm me — in fantasy, I mean. If I imagine that she hurt me, then I don't have to deal with how much I might want to hurt her.' Gina paused.

'Or how much I *have* hurt her,' she said.

'Here we go!' Patrick exclaimed. Gina threw up her hands in mock despair, laughing, as Patrick got up to clear the table. He went into the little kitchen to make the coffee. When he returned to the table, Gina was reading a book.

'There was this strange moment I never told you about,' Gina continued, putting the book to one side. 'That same time when I thought I was pregnant, and then my period came, violently, and I was so totally convinced I was having a miscarriage. You remember.'

'How could I forget?'

'Don't be mean. Anyway there was none of this let nature take its course routine, I was devastated, and filled with dread, you know, to have to go through it all again, and maybe miscarrying *again*, and suddenly, for one brief shining moment, in my desperation, I thought, if a doctor said, take this, and you won't miscarry . . . I would. For one moment, I occupied my mother's position, exactly, and I think that was when I forgave her, finally.'

A little later they were lying on the sofa, in each other's arms. 'I keep thinking about Harriet,' Gina said. 'I miss her.'

'Yes,' he said.

'But I keep thinking about how throughout her pregnancy she was completely obsessed with episiotomy.'

Patrick sat up. 'I've forgotten what that is,' he said.

'You know, where they make this neat cut, with scissors, at the bottom of the vagina, so it doesn't tear when the baby comes out, I mean, she was obsessed with tearing, the possibility of tearing, of being cut, and the question of being sewn up, and who would sew her up, and how. Like who was good at it, who was better, the midwife or the doctor, or what.'

'I guess it must be a bit like plastic surgery, irreversible. Someone sews up your vagina and maybe it's different to how it was before, and it *stays* like that.'

'That's right. *Horrible.* Though there's always stories of women lying there after giving birth, saying, make it nice and tight, doctor!'

'Wow.'

'Anyway Harriet was obsessed with this, and then I was talking to Stella on the phone yesterday, I was telling her about Harriet, and tearing, and Stella said, *absolutely.* That's one of the reasons, she said, that she never wanted to have a baby. As if the baby being born caused such unimaginable damage to the mother's body, she couldn't even bear to think about it.'

Patrick said nothing. Gina went on, 'Stella said Harriet must have really wanted the baby, to overcome her fears of having her vagina torn to pieces.'

'So it's the mother again,' Patrick said.

'I think it's about a certain kind of narcissism, a sense of identity almost, a kind of narcissistic fixation, that's based on this image of a vagina. You know, a perfect vagina, or maybe just, *my lovely vagina.* And I think how weird that is, because I've never thought, my lovely vagina. I don't think I've *ever* thought that. I've always thought, my no-good, damaged, odd, deformed, lacerated, weirdo vagina – that somehow has to manage, to make do. Because it's already damaged, in fact it's kind of a *mess* down there, and that's that.'

'So the lovely vagina, the perfect vagina is —'

'To me it's unimaginable, simply,' Gina interrupted. 'I can't really imagine how they would feel, Harriet, and Stella. Intact, maybe. Or something. I don't know.'

narcissistic disturbance

Above the desk, on the wall, there were two pictures. In one, Cézanne had painted a conch shell in such a way that it reminded Gina of a vagina. In the other, Georgia O'Keeffe had painted a cow's skull, with calico roses, in such a way that it reminded Gina of a vagina, a cunt.

Looking at one, then the other, hard and dry, sharp, the broken edges of the desert skull met the hard and shiny, cool contorted surface of the elaborate shell. The skull was white, the shell pink and red inside. A process of displacement, or metonymy, cunt to shell to skull, took place.

But cunts are wet and warm, not like this at all. The shell, the skull were (if they were) representations of vaginas that couldn't be fucked. As if they had the right qualities: elaborate interiors, a slit marking the opening where the inside and outside meet, the beautiful clitoris, undeniably there if you look for it, and that sense of further reaches, mysterious depths — this is the beginning place, the place of entry — but, not. The penis cannot penetrate this opening, it's too hard, too sharp. And the eye (blissful eye) can go no further, because a) it's a painting, flat, and b) you would have to cut or break the shell, the skull, to pursue this knowledge, to see the inner recesses of the object.

The shell was particularly beautiful because of the colours, and the curling forms which were like a baroque fantasy of a cunt. The skull was particularly satisfying because the structure of the head, the horns, recalled the triangular structure of uterus and ovaries. It was anatomically congruent, yet pushed as far from direct reference as it could be. Gina wondered if Georgia O'Keeffe thought of it as a cunt, a clitoris, and then she thought it didn't matter anyway, and anyway she probably did, of course she did. It goes without saying.

The shell was part of a still life that included some things that reminded her of penises, a row of erect penises in the folds in the linen, a flaccid penis in the glass vase. There was also a black clock without hands. It was impossible to imagine what Cézanne was thinking, consciously, when he made this painting.

Looking at one, then the other, *the unfuckable vagina*, Gina thought. Too hard, too shiny. The phallus, more or less.

cleavage

The other day I passed a decrepit movie theatre on Hollywood Boulevard; it was showing a double feature: *Faces of Death / Make Believe Is Not Enough*.

Let's face it, the body is always dying, on the verge of death — it's an embarrassment. The body is always embarrassing, and embarrassment is itself abject. The raw, the cooked, and the rotten — are we the rotten? Corrupt, diseased, deathly — fervently pursuing health or beauty while our cells rebel, metastasize, blossom into deathly flowers, or simply get tired.

Here in Los Angeles, the blank sun falls through poisoned air — air that destroys perspective, specificity of line and distance, in its unreal mist — this flat light falls on ideal bodies, hairless, muscular, on naked legs, bulky trainers and thick cotton socks, short denim skirts, bare midriff à la Madonna, endlessly permed hair. Every square centimetre of the body is tended, plucked, waxed, polished, inspected and adjusted. Exercise and liposuction and plastic surgery together keep it all in line, provide definition. Artifice is explicit in the heavy makeup (foundation, blusher, powder, lipstick, eyeliner, lipliner, eyeshadow, mascara) the women wear, despite the heat. Artifice is evident in the hair dyes, the perms, the cuts. Repeated exercises, supervised by personal trainers, reproduce identical muscles, ideal forms: the necessary dent in the upper arm, the sheer outline of a calf, a perfect thigh. Every body (almost) looks like this, each woman displaying the labour she has performed to make her body acceptable, ordinary. In this context, my pale, hairy legs are not merely an eccentricity, they're an abomination.

The other night I had dinner with a man who said he'd gone to a party in Beverley Hills with a bunch of very wealthy men and very pretty girls, and he'd thought, I don't want to tell these people I'm a writer, they couldn't care less about writers, in Hollywood writers are a dime a dozen. So he said he was a plastic surgeon. He said the women simply flocked to his side, he said they abandoned the promise of money for the promise of beauty, without hesitation. He said he was given what he called personal cards by six or seven beautiful women. He said that two of them, separately, had taken him upstairs, to show him their breasts. They both wanted to know: should they have had more?

I said, and what did you say? He said, I told them I thought they were fine.

Then he wrote an article about it. He talked to lots of women about why they'd done it, had silicone implants, and all of them said exactly the same thing: *so I could have a cleavage in a bathing suit.*

He said the problem with dating in LA is that as soon as you feel the silicone, it's not only unpleasant, unsexy, that is, but the woman also sort of falls in your esteem. What he said was, one thinks less of her, when one realizes.

I said, you can tell? He said, you can tell immediately.

He said, he couldn't help it, he thought less of the woman, invariably, because he thought, she must be so insecure, to do that to her body. I said, well I can sort of understand cutting bits off — actually I can't, but I find it even harder to think of inserting bits of plastic *into* your body. He agreed. I told him the last time I was in London, my older sister said, I'll never have plastic surgery, never, never, never, let's make a pact, we'll never have plastic surgery. And I'd said, sorry, I can't promise I won't! He nodded seriously, sympathetically, and said, well, yes, now you live in LA.

Another man I know told me, lovingly and amazed, almost reverentially, he told me that in labour his wife turned into an animal. Is that it? Is it birth, sex, food, shit that makes the body abject? What could be more abject than these breasts that continue to stand up even when you're lying flat on your back? They only work, they only look good when you're standing up, the man at dinner the other night told me. When you lie down, the fact that they don't sag is terribly disconcerting. Uncanny.

Or is it that all those things, food and shit and sex, are merely stand-ins for death — death which is always with us, just under the surface of the skin. All you have to do is make an incision, open a little door, and death springs out, red as blood, and grabs you by the throat. He's always there — like my grandmother used to say about men, she'd say, men are like streetcars, there's always another one just around the corner. That's where death is, just on his way, just around the corner.

such pleasures

Gina went round for a drink with Beatrix, who told her this story:

'It was said that what he really liked was fucking dead women. So the women who went out with him played dead.

'It would take some time to persuade them, one imagines, to talk them into it, but it was said that some of these women, the girlfriends, the lovely blondes, would submit to his will, or his wish. They would agree to be knocked out, in order to afford him these pleasures. They were all on drugs half the time, anyway, so maybe it wasn't such an extreme request, to suffer an injection and go under for an hour or two. Unconscious.

'He would administer the drug by injection, and then he would fuck her. And, it was said, that once the woman was out, unconscious, he would place her body in a freezer for a while — I imagine an enormous horizontal freezer in the larder or scullery next to the kitchen in his Mayfair flat, its coffin-like lid left open, her head sticking out, hanging over one end, as thin icy fog rises in wisps around her pale flesh.

'He would place her body in the freezer for a while, so that it would be cold when he fucked it. More lifeless, less lifelike. Less like a coma, more like dead.'

What Gina couldn't understand or imagine was how anyone could take pleasure in not knowing what was happening to them or what he was doing to them. It seemed an act of trust beyond her wildest dreams. 'How would you know you would ever wake up again?' she said. 'When he approached you with the hypodermic — no, this is taking masochism too far, this is beyond fantasy, much closer to an elaborate form of suicide, no?'

Beatrix was more comprehending. 'On the other hand,' she said, 'you have to admit, there's a tremendous power in giving pleasure up, in renunciation.'

She went on, 'And then supposedly he would be grateful, or something, for letting him do it to you, and he'd want to do it again. He'd stick around. It's called how to keep your man.'

On Splitting: A Symptomatology
or, The Los Angeles Maternal Position

1. Photograph

There was a photograph on the front page of the paper — *The Independent* — in London, early May 1992, when the baby was about three months old. It was a photograph that made Lee cry whenever she remembered it, and she remembered it quite often, she called it to mind, inadvertently, constantly. She couldn't talk about it with anyone at that time; she was embarrassed, awkwardly encumbered by these sobs, these floods of tears. She found it mysterious, the effect this photo had on her, and she didn't want to talk to anyone about it until she had this stuff more under control. Her emotion seemed like an obstacle, preventing her from understanding what might be at stake for her in this photograph. It was an obstacle she couldn't get through or over. Lee thought of the photograph, she wept, she tried to stop crying. The image would come to mind, tears would come to her eyes (as they did still, nineteen months later), and she would retire in perplexity, figuratively speaking, amazed by the intensity of this emotion and completely in the dark about its meaning.

It was almost as if the emotion rightfully belonged to someone else, or somewhere else. It seemed profoundly inauthentic, possibly, or maybe just inappropriate. The extremity of the emotion was undoubtedly inappropriate, if only because these ravaging tears interrupted the sweet flow of everyday, and then they exhausted her, the task of suppressing these inappropriate tears, these someone else's tears, tears from elsewhere, wore her out. It was profoundly inauthentic, it had to be, not least because the photograph represented a scene of starvation in Africa.

On the other hand, this seemed to be one of the acknowledged effects of motherhood: you weep over the morning paper, and can't watch the evening news. Was it that this emotion belonged rightfully to the mother, that other woman Lee was in the process of becoming? Who is this person? Lee thought. What is she doing invading me in this way, taking up residence in my head, transforming my body? The mother hadn't yet taken over completely — the mother never really does take over completely — she was still an alien element in Lee's psyche, which is why her tears seemed so strange. But it was like being faced with undeniable evidence of some part of her that was completely beyond her control: some incorporation, or impersonation, some strange other one taking her place.

Lee wondered why she hadn't kept the photograph. At another time in her life she wouldn't have hesitated: anything that had such an impact would be kept, salvaged, stuck in a file, slotted into the archives of her endlessly monitored, constantly changing subjectivity. And if she'd kept it, the photograph might have faded, so to speak, it might have lost some of its effect, from being viewed repeatedly. That's what repetition is for, to wear things down.

Lee could have looked at it, when she thought of it; it would have been something to do, some simple thing, to look at the photograph, when she was plagued with the question of what it was. She could have examined it for clues, for the detail that might give her attachment, her fixation, away, that lets it go. But the photo went out with the newspaper, into the chaotic heap in the hall, and though Lee sometimes thought of trying to retrieve it, she thought she could certainly go to the public library and find it, she never did. It was imprinted on her, it would remain there, inside.

The photo was taken in Somalia, before the US intervention there. The photograph showed a starving woman outside a Red Cross centre in Somalia. Her starving child was being weighed in a simple apparatus made up of a kind of triangular hammock or sling attached to a scale. The woman was turning away and she was smiling. This smile is impossible to describe. She was smiling as if the most wonderful thing imaginable had just happened.

A caption made it clear. She was smiling, it seemed, because the scales showed her baby to be under a certain weight, and the feeding centre would take the baby in, if it was under this weight. She was smiling because her baby was starving, and the child's weight was low enough for the Red Cross to take it in. She was smiling like this, she was so happy, because the baby would live. It was implied (Lee felt it was implied) that the child would live, or at least the child had a better chance, although (it was implied) she (the mother) might not, live, that is, or survive, and it was implied that in this situation, civil war, mass starvation, who could say if the woman would see this baby again, if she did survive, who could say if she would be able to find him, or her. She seemed bursting with energy, in that moment the photograph isolated, the moment when she understood, and turned away, glancing, leaving the baby there.

I can't describe the smile, Lee said. A baring of teeth, drawing back of lips, her eyes lit up with delight. I suppose it could be described as ecstatic. It was a grimace of bliss, her momentary glance towards the camera allowing me at my kitchen table in London to see, her look meeting mine across the immeasurable distance between us. When I thought of the photograph, when I wept those uncontrollable tears, Lee said, my nose running, my teeth clenched, a grimace of despair seized my mouth, stiffened my face. Her pain, her smile, was unbearable to me.

2. Armour

I didn't know why. My friend Bea is still in analysis — we all used to be in analysis, but then I packed it in — and she's super intense, and rather wonderfully always talking about the heaviest things. I went to see her at the end of the summer, before I left to begin this job teaching in LA, and we talked, about the past, mostly. And then I started, surprisingly, surprising myself, I started to tell her about the photograph in the paper, the photograph from Somalia, and inevitably I burst into tears, describing it to her. And Bea had to stand in for the lost analyst, again. First she was very sympa, and then she was curious, inquiring. She said, but what is it, what is it exactly about this picture? I mean, for you. It's awful — it's a terrible situation — but what do you think it means to *you?*

And I said, I don't know, I don't know. (I didn't know.) That the woman is giving the baby up, she's giving the baby away, she's so glad to be giving the baby away, because she loves it — not *despite* the love, but *because* she loves this baby, she's so happy, she's ecstatic. And Bea thought for a bit — we were walking in Ravenscourt Park, one of those smallish flat urban parks you get in London, with tarmac paths and a wading pool for the kids — and as we walked, I wiped my wet face with the heels of my hands, that bulge at the base of the thumb that fits so well into the eye socket, I felt that pressure, that contact. And then she said, do you think it's something to do with feeling that someone else could take better care of your baby than you can?

A revelation, of sorts. I can't protect her, I can't prevent her pain. I can't bear it. What is it that will harm her so? What must you protect her against? Me. Don't you think? It must be me. I mean, I'm the one who will do most harm — I'm her mother. So —what? — take her away from you? Take her away from me, keep her safe, may I never see her again, may I go away from her, keep her safe from me. For I will damage her, I am her mother.

Does this make sense? Does this ring a bell? All those women desperately trying to protect their kids — are they like me, terrified of the thing in myself that is capable of destroying everything good, that ravages, wreaks untold damage, leaves disaster behind?

Wreak, wrought. Overwrought. Highly strung. Maybe I'm

too highly strung for this. My mother always used to say, get down off your high horse. Which means something like, don't behave as if you're above all this, get down in the shit with the rest of us. She also used to say, rise above it. Rise above it, she'd say, when my sister tormented me. Climb back up on that high horse, and look down on her, on everyone, look down with contempt, immune, unscathed.

She emerged unscathed. She did not emerge unscathed. She was scathed by the image in the newspaper, scathed, or flayed, or pierced, her defences breached, or broached. A sore point, broached gently. She pictured it like medieval armour, remembering *Lancelot du Lac* of Bresson, the delicate task of inserting a poniard, a small dagger with a long, slender blade, between the armour, into the crack between the breastplate and the helmet, to pierce the throat. Locked in a deathly embrace, face to face, breathing hard, with the tremendous weight of the armour, and the narrow knife gradually wedged into the crack: a terrible, poignant, intimate killing.

The photograph undid her defences, found out the crack in her armour, pierced. The tears were hers, as (in fantasy) she gave her baby away — to anyone — because anyone would be better, anyone would be better than me.

3. Risk

So Lee understood something. The terrible, unspeakable danger — to her untouched, perfect, infallible baby — wasn't out there, it was in here. Of course there are dangers out there, but what can you do about it? she thought. Not a lot. You have to take risks, you have to walk down the street, you could get run over by a bus, but you have to walk down the street, a brick could fall on your head, someone could shoot you by mistake, the car could go out of control, the plane crash, whatever. None of the above. When Lee used to ride around on the back of motorcycles (at college her friends had motor-cycles and she was always riding around on the back), her mother said, well you know if you die, it's very sad, and we'll all go to the funeral and cry a lot, and then it's all over. But if you're in a wheelchair for the rest of your life — that's a *real* drag. Anything can happen.

What I have to do, Lee wrote, is to try to make sure that the bit of me that wants to protect the baby (from the part of me that will destroy the baby) (I think) doesn't ruin the baby's life.

The protective impulse is always only the other side of the destructive fantasy. And in a way it's infinitely more dangerous, because it appears to be 'good', it's socially sanctioned, it's proper mothering. I mean, this violence in me that is so great it will reduce the world to rubble, it will make the house explode, it will destroy everything, like an earthquake, like the refrigerator exploding at the end of *Zabriskie Point* — this violence is a fantasy. In some ways it may even be hypothetical, a construction of the analysis, as Freud would say. That is, buried so deep as to be surmised rather than experienced.

The reaction formation, the defence, is much more access-ible, in fact it's right there, on the surface, filtering everyday life, infusing domestic space, the outside world, presence, absence, the sunny garden, the bedroom, riddled with fear. Like a translation: rage turns into fear, a pendulum swinging from one extreme to the other. Protection, or protectiveness, is the symptom of fear, and fear only the reaction to this implicit violence, this death drive.

People do hurt their children. They break their arms and legs, they burn them on electric heaters, they beat them black and blue, and they beat them to death. Worse, beyond what I want to remember or imagine. I won't do that. I asked my Freud class, we were reading 'A Child Is Being Beaten', I asked if anyone there (about twenty people) had not been beaten by their parents. Silence.

Defence is always like a mirror, the other side of what is

being repudiated or fended off. Perhaps. But it seems clear that one is much less likely to murder the child, to throw the crying baby out of the window or to bash its brains out against the wall, than one is to terrify it with protective threats about a dangerous world. *It's not safe.* Poisoning the child with my own fears, making a ghastly clingy whiny fearful blighted mess — like me.

4. Contempt

Lee went to the first birthday party of a little girl down the street. (The child was one year old, but it was also Lee's first birthday party, her first children's birthday party, in LA.) Lee went, with Rose, and Rose wore her black dress with small red and blue flowers, and dark blue tights, and her green boots, terribly European. Rose was just beginning to walk, and as she came into the strange house, holding Lee's hand, the birthday girl tottered over and with her right hand reached out to scratch Rose's face, to the point of drawing blood. Rose stood there, stunned, not crying but amazed — no one had ever treated her like this — and Lee was amazed too, shocked, whereupon little Franny gave Rose a swift jab in the eye region with her left. It was the old one-two, translated into infant dimensions. Rose wailed, then, and Lee was ready to depart, but forced herself to stay, out of politeness. Rose recovered pretty quickly, and went outside to stumble around on the deck.

Lee knew no one; she stood still, surveying the scene: the hostess had made an enormous cake in the form of Big Bird; all the various foods and drinks were sugar-based; the other children, girls, were wearing flounced white dresses with white lace tights and black patent leather shoes; the other mothers seemed to spend an inordinate amount of energy shrieking at them to stay clean — but kids that age cannot stay clean, Lee thought, it's out of the question. Lee quickly discovered she was the only parent who sent her daughter to daycare; everyone else employed a woman from Central America, a 'housekeeper', a 'babysitter', except the frantic hostess, who was 'staying home' with hers. It was here that Lee had the conversation about the toilet lock.

She was talking to a woman with a lot of hair, dyed dark brown hair tied back and tumbling in curls down her shoulders and her back; a little fifties, Lee thought, a blast from the past. They were making conversation, tentatively, when the woman left, to go to the bathroom. She used the bathroom beside the front door — and moments later emerged, screaming, *you haven't got a toilet lock!*

The hostess, very apologetic, very flustered, said, we have them on the toilets upstairs, it's just that one, we always keep the door shut. Lee decided to have a real conversation; what is a toilet lock? she asked. It turned out it's a device to keep the tiny child from drowning in the toilet. Every home should have one — or three, as the case may be. Lee asked if anyone had ever even heard of a child drowning in a toilet. Lee said, I mean, if your second cousin ever knew someone who knew someone who lived around the corner from someone whose baby drowned in the toilet. Or if you'd ever read about it in the paper. If it ever happened. No. Still, they were a basic requirement, apparently.

Lee couldn't stand this stuff: child safety was now a massive industry, producing endless catalogues, each purveying a vast number of ever more elaborate devices to survey, control, and protect the infant. It was unthinkable not to have a baby monitor, so you never left the kid alone; it was unthinkable not to have drawer latches and locks for the fridge and gates on the stairs and guards on the stove and items to put on the hot bath tap and covers for the corners of every table and socket plugs in every socket. Lee did buy a lock for the VCR, so Rose couldn't stick Cheerios in it. But she was nauseated by the child-proofing syndrome, by this industry that preyed on people's fears. As if spending the money on some device, or on a houseful of devices, would somehow do the trick, bandage over the anxiety and the lack of control.

So she told the woman how she, Lee, hadn't child-proofed her house in any way, not even a gate on the stairs, and besides, she said, our parents never had all this gear, and we survived. The retort was deadly: I live in a much larger home than my parents did, the woman said, and my parents never left me alone all day with a — with a — here she faltered. With a woman from Central America? Of course, Lee wanted to say, they're *famous* for letting babies drown in toilets down there in Central America, silly me.

Now she was ready to leave, but there's an etiquette, a rule: you have to stay to watch the presents being opened. It's so you get to see the look of joy on the face of the birthday girl when she opens yours. So they stayed, even though the birthday girl didn't know she was supposed to look joyful; even though it was a party of tinies who were all high on sugar and chocolate and shrieking and fractious, and it had been going on for hours (two) and the kids couldn't keep it together much longer. Lee came away extremely depressed.

Walking home with Rose she picked up the mail: a padded envelope. They opened it and found a button cushion from Lee's friend Jane in London. She'd made one for her kid, and Lee'd admired it, and now here was a button cushion for Rose. It was about eight inches square, and on one face there were about forty different buttons — one like a clock, one like a teapot, a rose, an elephant, a racing car, etc. Different coloured buttons outlined the square. As an object, it seemed to imply a certain concentration of time and dedication: Jane searching in old shops to find these idiosyncratic, discontinued buttons, Jane maintaining the button collection, in boxes and little drawers, as well as Jane making the cushion, choosing, arranging, sewing them on. It was an object of contemplation, something a tiny child holds in its lap and studies. The button cushion was also, needless to say, potentially lethal, as kids choke to death on buttons all the time.

Ironically enough, one of the buttons did indeed come off within the first week — as if to prove how very un-Californian this object was. Lee sewed it on again, and wiggled all the others fiercely, to make sure. Matthew was amused by the toilet lock; he said, a baby would have to be both very intelligent and very stupid to drown itself in a toilet. The button cushion remained, part of everyday, to remind Lee of the toilet lock, and the hatred and loathing she felt, the insuperable distance between her and those other mothers.

5. Obstetrix

When I was pregnant, at the beginning, nine weeks, eleven weeks pregnant, I would weep, feeling that I couldn't protect the little transparent shrimp inside my belly. Protect it from what? I pictured doctors, technology, medical machines (I was trying to figure out amniocentesis), piercing my body, my body that should be protecting that little thing, that lively shrimp. Now I think it was the abortions, in my imagination, coming back to haunt me. Sharp instruments, doctors, and me — I'd chosen abortion, before, and now I felt I couldn't protect the foetus well enough, I couldn't protect it from those sharp instruments. And Bette said to Matthew, in New York, he told me she said, amnio is a wonderful thing — it allows older women to have babies without having to worry . . . The unconscious conflation of amniocentesis (my choice) and the abortifacient D & Cs (my choice) was countered by conscious thinking, a political decision. I was frightened of the amnio, frightened of miscarriage; nevertheless I shifted, I tried to shift my fears.

Amnio is a wonderful thing. I lay flat on my back and the doctor stuck the long long needle into my stomach just like you imagine someone stabbing you with a knife. He held it in his fist and shoved it down into my belly. First they have to draw out some of the fluid to clean out the needle, because of course the needle has gone through my skin and flesh, and has therefore been contaminated with my chromosomes. So they stick the long needle in, then they screw on a syringe and draw out some of the amniotic fluid, then they unscrew that one and screw on another, clean syringe, and draw out more fluid, this time pure, untouched amniotic fluid, which will contain only the foetal chromosomes. Then they pull the needle out, and it's all over.

Then the doctor put the ultrasound on again; he said, you see, the baby is still moving (a dancing shrimp with arms and legs), you see, there's still plenty of fluid for it. As if to say, you see, we didn't harm it, we really didn't.

I never thought I was going to die in labour. I mean, during labour, I never thought I was dying. It was afterwards that I thought I might be going to die. It crossed my mind; it had never crossed my mind before, and I've been very ill before, but I was in such bad shape, about two weeks after she was born, I had wild temperatures, up to 106, and so much sheer, unadulterated pain, and I didn't seem to be getting any better, and it crossed my mind that I might be dying. There was barely any emotion attached to this idea, as if I were really finally too tired to get upset about it, as if that in itself might be a sign that I might actually be dying. Women used to die in childbirth, or after childbirth, all the time.

Edward Shorter wrote a book called *A History of Women's Bodies*. It seems to me to explain feminism, the patriarchy, everything, pretty clearly. It goes like this: until recently — and in many places this is still the case — most women became pregnant and gave birth at regular intervals, more or less until it killed them. In this they had no choice. As a result, it was almost impossible for them to manage to do anything else, except cope with the appalling conditions of their lives. His descriptions of the complications, the instruments, the illnesses attendant on pregnancy and childbirth, are truly harrowing. In my view, until recently most women didn't have a chance to live the life of a human being. Their humanity was subordinate to the exigencies of reproduction.

6. Counter-phobia

There was an earthquake here. It happened on a holiday, a Monday. Martin Luther King Day: 4:31 a.m. As the day wore out, it became clear that we wouldn't be going to work this week; we wouldn't be pretending nothing had happened. (We had no electricity, so no TV, and no batteries for the radio, so we didn't know how bad things really were until the power came back on). It was hard to know what to do.

Rose goes to daycare in the Valley, exactly seven miles away from our house. I chose this daycare because Rita, who runs it, says things like, Rose you will have to learn to temper your passions with gentility! — as Rose, nine months old, on the floor, is trying to get as much of Christopher's hairless baby head into her mouth as she possibly can. Gentility, I thought, a four-syllable word flung out over the heads of babies — that's what I like about this place. I like her, I like the other kids, I like the way Rose never cries when I leave her at Rita's.

The epicentre of the earthquake was in the Valley too. Rita's is closer to the epicentre than our house, I think. I haven't measured, I haven't looked seriously at a map. But there were collapsed buildings all along the way to Rita's, and the park was full of tents and people sleeping in their cars, and the electricity and water were off, intermittently, though not at Rita's, her house was OK, and at 7:30 a.m. Tuesday morning she was open for business.

I didn't want to take Rose to Rita's on Tuesday morning. I didn't have to teach, to go to work, but we have so many tasks, letters, bills, taxes, that an unexpected day off work means we can get so much done! I didn't want to take Rose to Rita's, but Matthew took it for granted that Rose would go to daycare — or we didn't discuss it, I don't really know what he took for granted, but he never raised it as a question, and I believed that he thought it was the right thing to do. In any case, we went. Driving through the Valley early Tuesday morning was like driving through a scene of devastation. I was interested to note how very different one's response is to an actual collapsed building, especially a building one drives past every day, how very different that is to seeing collapsed buildings on TV, which are like all the other collapsed buildings, all the other disasters.

When I arrived at Rita's, it transpired that we were the only parents who'd brought our child to daycare — except for Dakota, whose parents had brought him because they'd lost their apartment, completely destroyed, and they were running around trying to find somewhere to live. What had we lost? Some plaster, a jar of honey and a jar of mango chutney that flew out of the kitchen cupboard, two bowls, a glass. Matthew's reading glasses were broken by a falling book, *Sigmund Freud and Art*, to be precise. We were very scared — or I was very scared. Matthew claimed not to be scared, but then his childhood memories are of the Blitz. (Later he did admit the whole experience was rather *stressful*). But he becomes David Niven circa 1942 in these situations, clutching Rose's toy flashlight, stalking around the house in the dark 'assessing the damage', going outside to try to find a radio, to find out some *news*, while the interminable series of aftershocks rolled through, and I held Rose in the dark in the doorway, immobilized.

We left our daughter at daycare in the Valley the day after the earthquake, while all the other parents, all the parents who had a choice, chose not to — and I felt mad, bonkers, out of control, like, how can I tell what is the right thing to do? I want to keep her here with me; I figure that's neurotic, that's crazy; I make myself take her to daycare, and discover *that's* crazy, that's something no one else is doing, if they don't have to.

It's counter-phobia, when you make yourself do something you're terrified to do. It's a compulsive act, beyond your control, the other side of the phobia itself. But separation anxiety is such that every ordinary everyday farewell is in some measure counter-phobic.

Around the corner from where we live a house fell down the side of the mountain in the earthquake. A man and a woman were trapped; she was seven months pregnant and her pelvis was broken. Their four-year-old daughter was killed. The parents were taken to different hospitals. *We lost her*, the man said.

So I go on taking Rose, saying goodbye, easily, easily, take it easy, I say, because I have to, take it easy, because you can't hold on to them, it only ruins things for them and it doesn't necessarily even keep them safe.

My friend said it was hard for her to begin to say *no*, to actually say the word *no* to her one-year-old, so she said she had taken up saying *it's not safe*. I said, but that just portrays the world as a terrifying, dangerous place, a place full of danger. She said she hadn't thought of that. Then I remembered how hard it was for me, to begin to say no, and I wondered what it was about. It's such a pleasure when the kid's only tiny, that infancy thing, where you don't refuse, you only say yes. You scoop the baby up if it's about to fall or hurt itself, but you deny it nothing. Is it that we don't want to be hated, the wicked witch, the agency of prohibition? (He may symbolize it, Daddy, I mean, but we live it out.) We want to say yes, to be loved, the endless cornucopia, and instead we find ourselves saying no, not now, stop, stop that right now, that's enough, I won't have that, that's enough, and even, occasionally, that's not safe. I love taking risks with Rose, that is, allowing her to take risks — I love it because I can see how she feels the world is a good place, full of adventure and delight. I don't want to cramp her style. I don't want her to be scared.

So I take her, and leave her, despite the aftershocks, despite my own separation anxiety. Cut off my own nose to spite my face, to make it good, to make it all right. When the aftershocks come she stands still in the middle of the room, utterly surprised, and I say, it's all right, it's all right, it's all right. There's an element of counter-phobia in every farewell, every good-night. Like all mothers, I have listened in her dark bedroom to make sure she's breathing; I've imagined her dead, face down in the bath. Recently I moved my collection of kitchen knives (razor-sharp Sabatiers) out of the kitchen drawer and into a glass vase on the kitchen counter — my first gesture of baby-proofing. She's tall enough now to get things out of the drawers, and as I stood in the shower, allowing her to roam through the empty house, I would fantasize a scream (you can't hear anything in the shower except possible distant screams), I would picture her holding the ten-inch chopping knife over her head, a tiny Attila, charging around the kitchen, and the knife falling and cutting her. Babies bleed to death very quickly because their heartbeat is extremely fast and they have very little blood inside their bodies. Comparatively. That's my theory, anyway. That a baby would bleed to death very quickly.

My sister cut her jugular vein on a broken glass when she was two. Her life was saved by a friend of my mother's who knew where to press. They'd been playing bridge, I think, four women and their toddlers, and my mother was saying, oh my daughter is very good, she never climbs up on things, when they heard a crash from the kitchen and ran in to find my sister bleeding to death. She'd climbed up on the kitchen table, with a glass of orange juice, and fallen off. I picture bright orange and red liquid on the shiny linoleum floor. The doctor said she wouldn't have survived if they'd arrived at the hospital thirty seconds later.

So I put the knives away, out of reach, and continue to take hurried showers, listening, listening for her screams.

7. Hatred and loathing

Why should I hate it so much, the toilet lock, the mother who's upset when the kid gets dirty, or who makes more of a fuss than the child when the kid falls over or bumps her head? Ouch! she says, before the kid's had time to decide whether it's painful or not. Hug, she says, hug, as the kid's ready to wander off, do something else. I hate it because that's me, that's the overprotective, let me fix it for you, kiss it better, hug, never lay a hand on her, no, no one will ever lay a hand on her, let us be all in all to each other, true love forever and ever, you're mine, swallow you up, all mine, never let you go bit. It's the bit that wants to keep her clinging to me, in my arms, to keep her safe, with me, always. Rita laughed with me about how I'd feel when Rose went out on dates; I said, Dates! Never! You must be joking!

It's the bit I won't give in to, the bit I suppress, because I know it would ruin her life, ruin my life, ruin everything. So it drives me crazy when I see other women doing it, letting themselves do it, doing what that bit of me wants to do so much.

8. Theory

What she wanted to write about was splitting. So she looked it up in the dictionary of psychoanalysis.

Laplanche and Pontalis on the paranoid position theorized by Melanie Klein:

a. *As regards the instincts, libido and aggressiveness (oral-sadistic instincts: devouring, tearing) are present and fused from the outset . . .* *

*cf. my constant return to the word ravage, ravaging, ravaged.

b. *The object is partial, its prototype being the maternal breast.* *

*i.e., me, the mother, the good or bad breast, but I'm still the infant, too, somewhere, and my little one, my own infant, is also a part-object for me — in fantasy.

c. *This part-object is split from the start into a 'good' and a 'bad' object, not only inasmuch as the mother's breast gratifies or frustrates, but also because [the infant] projects its love or hate on to it.*

*The part-object (which slots into the psychic equation breast=penis=faeces=baby =money=gift) itself always has two sides, cuts both ways. Split from the start.

d. *The good and bad objects which are the outcome of this splitting attain a relative independence of one another, and each of them becomes subject to the processes of introjection and projection.*

*A relative independence: when the 'good' and 'bad' objects no longer hold together, but fly apart, like atoms, like opposing magnetic poles, radically separated, because any contact, any contamination or combination between them is simply too anxiety-provoking.

e. *The good object is 'idealized': it is capable of providing 'unlimited, immediate and everlasting gratification'. Its introjection defends the infant against persecutory anxiety . . .*

*My baby is the good object idealized: unlimited, immediate and everlasting gratification.

The bad object, on the other hand, is a terrifying persecutor; its introjection exposes [the infant] to endogenous threats of destruction.

*Endogenous threats: the thing in me that will blow up the world, the house, the baby.

f. *The ego . . . has only a limited tolerance of anxiety. As means of defence, aside from splitting and idealization, it uses denial (disavowal), which seeks to divest the persecuting object of all reality, and omnipotent control of the object.*

*Disavowal and control: the danger lies elsewhere, because I am the (all powerful) good mother to this (inviolate) good baby. I can even leave the sharp knives loose in the kitchen drawer — because (magical thinking) nothing can happen to us.

g. *'These first introjected objects form the core of the super-ego.'**
*Super-ego: my mother told me she'd given the persecutory voice in her head a name. She said, you know, that voice that tells you you're no good, not good enough, how terrible you are — I call her Auschwitz. I say (my mother said), I say: *Shut up, Auschwitz!*

9. Notes on splitting

I don't know how to approach this topic, splitting; I don't even necessarily agree with Melanie Klein (who invented the paranoid position), and I think dear old Laplanche and Pontalis aren't wildly sympathetic to her either. All I know is I live in fear of destroying everything, and therefore hold things together compulsively, trying to make good the destruction that I feel I must have (on some level) already carried out, or maybe that I am (unconsciously) continually carrying out, wreaking, all the time. And I live in fear of my 'good' object, the baby, being hurt or damaged or destroyed; I feel it would kill me, it would be unbearable.

But most of all, I think, I feel I deserve to be persecuted, for being so happy. I have banished evil from my world (more magical thinking), and so it must be out there lying in wait for me. And in my experience, making artwork is aggressive and destructive and violent and painful, and it hurts me and hurts others, and these days I feel like there can be no possible justification for that pain, for that writhing around on the floor, that anguished gnashing of teeth. I don't know how to hold the baby to the 'good' breast, so to speak, while my pen (black ink, bad breast) spews insight, invective, cruel, cutting, incisive words. I am paralyzed, immobilized, stuck in the gap between the two: bad-girl artist, good mother. Incompatible, incommensurable, incompetent. Faced with this particular conflict, I shut down, and desperately find reparatory work to do, 'compulsive repetition of reparatory acts' (like teaching? folding the laundry?) — or else resort to delusion, what are called manic defences, also known as feelings of omnipotence. I feel like I could disappear, fall off the planet, never answer the phone, never open a letter. It's phobic — as if I could sidestep the aggression in me, or smother it, and ignore the danger out there, if I just keep my head down, and go on, insistently, gazing into the baby's eyes.

Unfortunately, the baby persists in growing up, and won't lie still. I need a place to hide, a phobic bolt-hole, and she won't play, she wriggles in my arms, she scoots off, interested in something else: rabbits. I'm left with this emotional baggage, this terror of just retribution — it's not persecution, it's more like punishment I anticipate; I think it's the price I have to pay for my writing, for the baby. So I'm left with compulsive repetition of reparatory acts and manic defences: denial, idealization, splitting, or omnipotent control. My armour, designed to keep the baby safe.

10. Out of the labyrinth

It was a conundrum; Lee felt trapped. She couldn't get past her terror, her fear that the child would somehow be lost or harmed, and she would be powerless to prevent it, or worse, she would be the source of that harm.

It was no comfort to insist, as Lee insisted, that this was indeed the case, nothing to be frightened of, nothing to worry about, simply a fact of life. Parents damage their children, it's unavoidable. Growing up is a process of being damaged by the world, Lee thought. The idea was excruciatingly painful.

You can earthquake-proof your house, the way you baby-proof your house, but that won't fix it, quite. Lee's memory of the photograph of the woman in Somalia was still beyond her control. Lee knew her response to the photo was about her own fears; she knew it had nothing to do with the Somali woman's experience, which Lee could only begin to imagine. The earthquake was a real danger — theoretically, although like all the other threats, it seemed finally only to stand in for Lee's violence, her anxiety. Matthew said he never imagined the world to be a *safe* place. He was pretty fatalistic about it. Look at European history, he said, you can't look at what happened in the last century and imagine you'd be *in control*.

Lee's mother phoned, a few days after the earthquake. Lee told her about it; she'd been scared to death, she said. It's the emotional repercussions, she said, and the aftershocks, that go on and on and on. Lee's mother talked for a while longer, then she said, but you sound a little *subdued*. As if to say, reassure me, tell me you're all right really. Lee was irritated, even hurt, but when she thought about it later, she saw how that wish to protect the child, to deny all danger, all sorrow and harm, would persist — despite everything. And how intolerable it would be to be so powerless, thousands of miles away, and to hear about the scenes of devastation, the aftershocks, the terror. How you might say, tell me it's OK really, because I just can't bear the thought that it's really not.

Lee felt stuck, trapped. Then she discovered there was a way out — that it is the child who leads you out of this trap, out of this bubble of maternal preoccupation, this enclosed world, out of the compelling fantasy of being all in all to each other, of being *good*. The child leads you out, magnificently, by becoming a human being, and therefore (like all human beings) subject to conflict, torn apart by internal strife. As if this thing one wants so much to repudiate, this 'bad object' banished forever, shows up again in the gleaming eye of the tiny tot intent on destruction, and you have to laugh, you have to let it go, give it up. The child won't stay locked in the perfect bubble — she wants to go make something happen, she has something to say, she wants to be by herself.

You can have another baby, Lee thought, you can try to prolong this state of affairs, this unlimited, immediate and everlasting gratification. Then you'd have to have another one, and another.

Or you can take cover, and let everything go, and hang on to the memory, that indelible image of the good child, the good mother, inseparable.

Or you can let the child bring you back — to language, to violence, and to that tired, fallible, damaged body — not to rush in panicky with the quick fix, compulsive as ever, but slowly, with difficulty, to make it good.

Separations

1. Wishful thinking

What we think about when we think about loss.

Viktor Shklovsky and the crossed out letter in *Zoo*; Jacques Lacan and the grapheme of The Woman crossed out; Carrie Fisher and her letters to the baby yet unborn. The unborn is a term from the abortion debate in the US; the unborn is what they're fighting over. The unborn is hypothetical, it's ideological. The unborn sounds like the undead to me.

Apparently in Japan, women's life expectancy is something like six years longer than men's, and therefore the aged widow is a regular thing, and she has her own derisive nickname, *ribojin*, which means 'not yet dead person'. As if that didn't apply to all of us.

I'm amused almost by the virulence of this wish for a baby. As if it's still the *baby* that I wish for, that inimitable thing, the baby, even though I've had one. I wished for a baby for what — for five years, or something, and then, amazingly, I got to have a baby, and I had the baby for about eighteen months, there was the baby, and I was ecstatic, and then gradually the baby vanished, replaced by an extremely lovely little girl, and I love her, and I'm left with the wish for a baby again. A virulent wish: poisonous, having a rapid course and violent effect.

In Victorian families, the youngest child was called the Baby, or Baby, and it slept in the mother's bedroom until it was (inevitably) dislodged by the next baby. Whereupon it would begin to be addressed by name. This interests me — infant mortality was so high, perhaps the Baby didn't really require a place in the social, a name of its own, until it had successfully run the rapids of infancy. Names which had been given to babies who died were often reused, or recycled, and given to babies born later. So you'd have Amelia I, Amelia II, and sometimes even Amelia III, in the same family.

Being a good mother meant keeping your baby alive, skills which we've more or less handed over to the doctor and the pharmacist. It's taken for granted now that mothers don't know anything, that they don't have to know anything, really. It's taken for granted, almost, that babies don't die. The relentless sequence of pregnancies also meant there was no need to wean the baby, to get it to give up the breast, because the mother's milk dries up when she becomes pregnant again. So that marker of the transition from infancy to early childhood was non-negotiable, so to speak, it was out of their control.

Alternatively, maybe the baby was called the Baby because that's what it was — and a name was only felt necessary when the little mite itself began to use language, to stop being a baby.

My friend Julie's mother is seventy-eight, and she acquired a puppy, and Julie talked to her on the phone, and said, 'How lovely to have a puppy,' and her mother replied, 'I'd rather have a baby.' Julie has five sibs, her mother had six kids, and she's seventy-eight, and she'd rather have a baby. Julie said to me, 'See, it never ends. *Never!*' This seems like a truly dreadful prospect. Years of doomed longing stretch before me, the vibrant fantasy ever beckoning, vivid and undeniable.

My sister said, 'It's easier to get over it when it's not possible. As long as it's a possibility, I think you'll be thinking about it.' Another dreadful prospect. I don't want to go on thinking about it. I want to do it, and get it over with, get on with it, or else decide not to do it, and get over it.

At a certain point, the baby becomes a child, and the child delights. Nevertheless, you want the baby again, another baby. And part of the point of the fantasy is to make good this loss — the baby that has become a child, and will never be a baby again. E. is two, and she plays at being a baby, she has done all summer, since she left daycare. She began by climbing into my arms to lie cradled there, making baby noises, which sound like a puppy whining. She says, 'Babies can't talk.' Then in a high voice she says, 'Me want to nurse,' and she strokes my breasts, or reaches down my neck to touch them. This is outrageous: we never called it nursing, that's an Americanism, and besides we quit months ago, and she's never shown the least sign of regret. This is all a game for her — not for me.

Nursing is what her dearest friend at daycare calls it; Louise is older than E., and she's still doing it. Her mother says Louise has given each breast a name, and plays complicated fantasy games with them; one imagines a kind of reverie in which both mother and child partake while lying in bed together, nursing. Then Louise talks about it the next day to the other two-year-olds, and when her mother comes to pick her up at the end of the day, she says, 'I want to nurse.' Louise speaks perfectly grammatical English and has done since she was about eighteen months old. She says things like, 'After my sandwich, I would like to have some ice cream.' It's uncanny. Anyway, I thought E. was just copying Louise.

I don't like the term 'nursing'. It has lousy connotations for me. It's like this word 'comfort' the baby books use all the time, as a euphemism for pleasure. I call it breastfeeding, and I used to say to the baby, do you want a suck? That seemed closer to what was actually going on, although it's too simple to say what's going on is sex.

I was always available, I mean, the breast was always available, whenever I was around. Such an odd expression, the breast, as if the definite article somehow makes safe this sexual object, this extraordinarily useful thing. As if to take two individual, idiosyncratic breasts and refer to them as the Breast, like the Queen, or the Ukraine, is to elevate the lowly object, to make it impersonal and somehow absolute. Like the Baby, indeed. Anyway, the breast was offered, by me, constantly, casually, when I was around, as if it really wasn't a big issue whether the baby sucked or not. A friend hypothesized that a truly insecure neurotic mother wouldn't be able to offer the breast in this easygoing way, because half the time it would be rejected. (That's the other virtue of calling it 'the breast', you can refer to it as it, instead of she.) Half the time, she would be rejected, and that would be intolerable. But I was easy, as they say.

These days, when E. says she wants to nurse, I talk to her. 'My breasts are empty,' I say, 'there's no milk in there.' 'You're not a baby any more,' I say, 'you're a big girl.' And lately, I say, 'Don't play with my breasts. I don't like it.' 'You no like it?' she says, looking up at me. 'Me like it,' she asserts, amused by my troubled face. If I make a fuss, it makes it more of an issue, and she'll fight with me. If I don't make a fuss, I have this two year old climbing into my lap and shoving her hands down my bra. I smile and say, 'Don't play with my breasts, please.'

It's continued now for a couple of months, and partly I feel like I'm being taunted, because I was the one who breastfed her on demand for fifteen months, and who continued with two lengthy feeds a day until she was twenty-one months old. I was the one whose breasts were never empty, who was easygoing and generous and available, when I was around. Now, at thirty months, two and a half years old, she doesn't say, 'Me want to nurse,' any more, she says, 'I want to play with your breasts.' She's taken up my expression, she's taken me at my word. When I say no, she says, 'I *want* to.'

For the child to return to the breast as some kind of elaborate joke, a sexy game, is like an old lover turning up and climbing into bed with you. For the ex, it's a whim, a little bit of nostalgia, a flingette. For you, it's heartbreak. Don't play with my heart, I want to say, don't play with me this way.

What was once our daily intimacy, our lovemaking, is now her silly game. My friend Annie says breastfeeding is analogous to sex, in that you know when you're having good sex and when you're having bad sex, and you have to think about it, and work it out, and at the same time, somehow, figure out how to relax and enjoy it. Breastfeeding was our intimacy, our consummation — and now it's something to be referred to, to be discussed, I guess. It's mediated by an idea that she's got from somewhere else, from Louise, her pal at daycare, that seems to me to have very little to do with the thing itself. It's like she's seen it, she's seen other kids doing it and she thinks it would be fun. Because I don't think she can possibly remember it, I don't think she can remember that time. She wasn't talking then.

It's partly a question of language, as if talking about it isn't it. As if part of the pain of the child acquiring language and not being a baby any more is giving up that intense, non-verbal, non-mediated relation. I used to believe that sex was like that, that sex was not a signifier, it didn't mean anything at all, it didn't refer to anything but itself. I don't know if I still think that, after all these years of sleeping with the same person. Because the value of sex now appears to be what it might mean, that we still love each other enough to try to give and take pleasure in that way. Or that we love each other enough to try to have a baby. Or that we don't.

You think about it, and try different things, and watch and hold the baby, to follow the baby's response. You use your mind and your body to make it good, for both of you, and when you get it right it seems so easy, it's a breeze. When it doesn't work, when the baby's crying and you try everything and nothing makes it better, you want to shoot yourself. Some babies are like that a good part of the time, it's called colic. It doesn't last forever.

What I remember is that gesture, when you bend your elbow in, to push the side of your breast with the palm of your hand, to feel which one is more full. I remember giving a reading when E. was three and a half months old, and realizing I was meant to be on stage at the very moment when I was unbuttoned, unzipped, and she was sucking away. I heard the applause stop, and I realized that was for the previous person, I realized I was supposed to be on stage. I flew.

I remember all the gigs I did when she was in the audience, and how Robert would take her out into the hallway when she cried, she cried when she heard my voice, usually, and how divided I felt. I remember when she was a year old I had a gig to do and I left her with Julie, and I performed well for the first time since she was born, because she wasn't in the building, because I'd forgotten about her completely.

Julie said she knew it was time to pack it in when her son would let go of her nipple and croon, 'Other side! Other side!' The baby drains one breast, and wants the one on the other side, the one that's still full. She felt if he could ask for it, it must be time to quit.

E. says, 'Me got no breasts.' We tell her she has little breasts, she has nipples, and when she's big she'll have bigger breasts, and maybe she'll be a mummy someday too. She's delighted with this, she says, 'Me a mummy,' and puts her baby doll to her chest, making baby noises. Then she says to Robert, 'You have nipples?' He concedes this fact. In the restaurant, out of the blue, E. cries delightedly, 'Me have nipples, me have nipples!' To my sister, she said, 'You have big breasts, you not my uncle, no.' Big breasts, little breasts, nipples. She talks about vaginas and penises too, but apparently the breast is still the crucial thing. The breast is the mark of difference.

2. Champagne

My mother's idea about breastfeeding was it was too good for the baby. 'Breastmilk is like champagne,' she cried, as if to say, only for special occasions. We argued, often, during the pregnancy, and gradually I recognized an ancient paradigm: the dinner party, my mother's beaded brocade knee-length fitted dinner dress, her sheer stockings, bright silk high heels. My mother implicitly believed that men only stuck around (and let you have your babies, or their babies, rather) if you bounced right back — hurtling out the front door to the formal dinner, hair done, made up, with no sign of maternal disruption, no leaky, engorged breasts, no heavy hips, and no irrational longings, no intense, unspeakable attachment to the three-week-old thing, the little omelette, the little scrambled *objet*.

Miss Jolly took care of me for the first six weeks, and my inability to catch — anything: balls, frisbees, cigarette lighters — was always put down to the hilarious fact that Miss Jolly dropped me on my head, once.

In any case, when the baby, my baby, was born, and she was enormous, and I phoned my mother, and I said: 'It's a girl, she's enormous, eleven pounds, three and a half ounces' — without hesitation, my mother said: 'You'll *never* be able to breastfeed that child!' The first thing, first response was this dark echo of a distant curse, some voice of doom from beyond the 1950s, a voice of prohibition, drawing the line: No, you can't have a baby and have *that* too.

Harriet says they're jealous, simply, our mothers. The child-care culture of their day insisted that doing anything 'on demand' was exceedingly harmful to the baby, giving it a feeling of omnipotence that it just couldn't handle. One must stick to schedules, rigorously, one must train the child in self-control, preparing it for a world of delayed gratification.

We think the opposite now. We think meeting the baby's demands gives it a sense that it lives in a good world, where needs and demands can be responded to and met. We think the sense of power this gives the baby is healthy, we think we are respecting the baby as a human being right from the start. We think we are helping the baby to learn how to communicate: the baby cries, we comfort it. We respond. When my mother's babies cried, she ignored them. That doesn't seem right, these days.

I was fine, apparently, an easy baby, and then my mother told me I developed colic when she quit breastfeeding at one month. Then I was fine, except when I was screaming the house down. She said, nothing could comfort you, nothing.

I suspect, absurdly, that our way of doing things is harder on the mother — although clearly my mother's domestic arrangements, for example, weren't what you might call easy. It seems as if it's always really hard whatever you do. It's unbelievably difficult, and at the same time, paradoxically, the most pleasurable thing ever.

When E. was born, I thought, wow! So this is what all those women incomprehensibly living in the suburbs have been doing — having babies! I felt like I'd become a member of a secret society, a group who all knew firsthand how amazing this thing was, who knew how it wasn't represented anywhere, this thrill, this pleasure, superseding all previous pleasures, all other activities.

I was almost shocked the other day when I was talking with a friend, an old friend that I hadn't seen for a long time; we were talking about the boyfriends, we were griping, inevitably, and she said, 'It's always *me* that has to think, that's the last banana, we're out of cheese, I've got to do the laundry, the baby's run out of socks, etc.' So we were commiserating, and I was saying, 'I don't know a single household where this is not the case,' when she said, suddenly, shocking me, she said: 'But how *could* they be as involved as we are, I mean, they don't have the same contact, do they?' I looked at her. 'Let's face it,' she said, gesturing towards her eighteen-month-old son, 'I get much more out of this relationship than I ever could with any *man.*' And I thought, she said it. She said it out loud, she said the unsayable thing.

3. Childbirth

It may be impossible to describe labour. I've tried, in writing, and it may simply be the degree zero of women's experience, something which can be referred to, gestured towards, but never written. And who would be interested? Women who've done it, women who are about to do it, maybe. It might mean something to them. It's very isolating, thinking about it; I feel very alone with the memory of it, as if the quality of the experience is impossible to convey, and as if it's impossible to know what it meant to me.

I suppose it always means the same thing: this tremendous thing, this new baby. It's all about her. As if I wasn't alone with it, after all, but it was something we did together, E. and I, to get her into the world. As if she had to be strong, and keep going, and I had to be strong, and keep going, and we had to get through it somehow, and we did. People usually do. On the other hand, she doesn't remember it like I do.

I can't describe it. The pain filled me up, it filled my whole body, and it reduced the world to a small part of the darkened room, the space between the bed and the window, where I was, with this pain. Robert was there too, at the edge of my consciousness, and Sharon, the labour nurse, and the pitocin drip was there, a pump on a stand that had to be plugged into the wall. The pump's battery didn't work, so we couldn't move around much at all. The drip went into the back of my left hand, a long needle taped to my hand in such a way that I couldn't bend my wrist. This meant that I couldn't kneel, because I couldn't support myself on my hands. I couldn't squat, because I couldn't support myself, because I couldn't bend my wrist back. I couldn't lie down, the pain was too intense, I had to keep moving. So I was on my feet, hour after hour, breathing.

The window was a sliding window, and it was way below freezing outside, night time, frozen snow on the ground. I wanted air, lots of air, but it was so cold outside I could only have the window open half an inch. Still, I focused on that crack, as if the fresh air was everything. On the window-sill was the little boombox, and the cassette tape that we played over and over and over again: Thelonius Monk. We brought a bunch of tapes to the hospital but that was the only one that worked for me. Somehow the precision of the piano, the relentless, deliberate sequence of each note, kept me there, gave me something to hang on to. When it was time to turn the tape over, I almost lost it, I couldn't keep it together unless those notes were playing. All night long, incessant, over and over again, we listened to Thelonius Monk play. I forgot everything, the world became that window, my breath, the sound of that piano playing. The pain filled me up, erased the world. With every single contraction they had to talk to me, they said, relax, breathe, relax, breathe, breathe, relax. Every single one, all night long, Robert and Sharon talked me through it. I didn't look at them, I heard their voices beside me, I was swaying from side to side, shaking my head, breathing out.

I forgot everything, I forgot there was such a thing as anaesthesia, I forgot there was any kind of alternative. I was in this thing, I wasn't on top of it in any sense, I was inside it, and all I knew was I had to get through it. I had this determination to get through it, and a kind of stubborn short-sightedness. I couldn't see any further than the next minute, the next thirty seconds. The doctor kept turning up the pitocin, they adjust the pump and the contractions come faster and they get stronger. It was like being tortured. I remember standing, dancing, moving my limbs, my knees bent, my arms shaking out the pain, and breathing, breathing deep and slow. On the window was my plastic cup of Evian water with Rescue Remedy in it. There was nothing else.

This went on for twelve hours or so. I'd already been doing the gradual, gentle beginnings of labour at home for about sixteen hours before that. The waters broke at six a.m., and by seven p.m. the contractions were erratically coming about every five minutes. It wasn't unbearable. I went to the hospital at nine, and the contractions stopped completely. I hated the doctor, I hated having to go to the hospital. The doctor said I had to do pitocin, and by ten p.m I'd unhappily agreed. All night long the contractions came, one after the other, with no space between them, no breathing space. The contractions were longer than the space between them, all night long. Sharper, deeper, longer, as they turned the pitocin up, all night long.

With every contraction I pictured a red flower opening, my cervix opening, a red rose. I never spoke about it to anyone. At one point, Sharon said to me, 'Ride it like a wave,' and all my most ancient terrors, uncontrollable fears of the vast, fathomless ocean, rushed in. I was absolutely terrified, momentarily. My worst nightmares are nightmares of scale, when the waves are beyond measure, the sea unimaginably deep. I believe these terrors are the terrors of infancy, where there are no boundaries, no above and below, left and right, no walls, floors, ceilings, just flight, and sudden landing, beyond your control. Picked up, put down, falling, in thin air. Studies have shown that a newborn baby recognizes a drawing of eyes, mouth, nose as a face, no matter where they are placed in relation to each other. The mouth can be above the eyes, and the baby still responds, and it makes sense, because there can be no above and below for the infant, everything is all at once and in any order, without form. Sharon said, 'Ride it like a wave,' and I was flooded with fear, lost at sea, alone in a vast ocean. 'No,' I said. 'I can't.' I went on listening to Thelonius Monk, picturing the red rose opening.

At six a.m. it was still dark outside. They told me to push. They told me I was fully dilated, time to push. This was like going to hell. I tried, I said, 'I can't push,' they said, 'Then you'll have to have a caesarean.' I pushed, hard, for three hours.

I pushed standing up, I pushed sitting on the toilet, I pushed holding on to the bed. Breathing through a contraction is all about letting go, letting the pain shimmer through your body, releasing the pain, as you shake your hands and fingers, sway from side to side. I'd become pretty good at this. Pushing, on the other hand, is all about holding the pain in, holding your breath and holding onto the pain and directing it all downward as hard as you can. It was like turning everything inside out, all my skills, my deep breathing, releasing, had to become the opposite: I had to learn how to hold on to the contraction, to shit it out, instead of letting it go. It was hell.

At ten a.m. the sun was pouring into the room, and we decided, somehow, during the contractions, it was decided that I had to have a caesarean. I was convinced by Sharon, she showed me the chart, she told me the baby had descended precisely one and a half stations during the previous twelve hours, despite the pitocin, despite the pushing, and there were six more stations to go. The baby was nowhere near being born. Somebody turned off the music.

I trusted Sharon completely, and she was quite clear that the caesarean was necessary. I asked Robert what he thought and he said, 'I think it would be nice to meet the baby.' As soon as the decision was made, I wanted the contractions to stop. If the contractions weren't going to bring the baby, I couldn't stand them another second.

They produced a form for me to sign, and they turned off the pump, and shaved my pubic hair. The pitocin was still circulating in my bloodstream, still generating the occasional contraction, unbelievable, irrelevant pain. At eleven I was in the operating theatre, laughing with the anaesthetist, joking with the five student nurses who were observing the operation, shaking hands with the paediatrician. It was like a party, people kept arriving, introducing themselves; in the end there were sixteen people packed into this bright little room. The two doctors talked the student nurses through it, a running mono-logue, 'Now we're making the first incision, this is the really hard part, because if you go too far you puncture the bladder, there's the amniotic fluid, now, ladies, what colours can we expect amniotic fluid to be?' 'Green,' one said, 'or brown.' 'Clear,' said another. Listening, it was like a radio play, and I was stunned to think that we were finally going to have this baby, for good or ill. In that moment, I turned my face to Robert, I wanted him to tell me he wanted to have a baby. It seemed absurd to ask him, and there wasn't time, suddenly she was out of there, screaming and wriggling and the biggest girl baby anyone had ever seen. She had bright red hair and a crooked foot, and all the student nurses cried out: 'Strawberry blonde!'

Robert said afterward that I was like someone who has been given the most wonderful, most unexpected present. I was ecstatic; my happiness is impossible to describe.

4. Despair

I was always very struck by how everyone who had a baby in California talked about Ferberization. 'We Ferberized Harry when he was four months old,' Harry's mother would say with a smile, 'and we haven't heard a peep out of him since!' When met with my perplexed incomprehension, they would excitedly explain there is a book, a key book, by Dr Ferber, which provides exact instructions on how to get your baby to sleep through the night. They were evangelical — these conversations took place even while I was pregnant — and when I understood, I felt their excitement had all the signs of anxiety and guilt, evidence of a desperate wish to include me, and all parents, in the Ferberizing group, a wish to eradicate the lingering suspicion that there must be another way.

It goes like this, apparently: you put the baby in its bed, kiss it goodnight, and leave. Or actually you have a rather elaborate bedtime ritual with bath, pyjamas, stories, goodnight to family photos, teddy bears, dolls. This is followed by the kiss goodnight and the parents' departure. The child is warm, well fed, and comfortable. Needless to say the child cries. You wait exactly ten minutes, then you go back in, both parents preferably, to demonstrate that you are both there. You talk to the child, reassuringly, but you do not hug or kiss the child, or take it out of its bed. You do not breastfeed the child, or offer it anything other than a drink of water. In other words, you do nothing to reward the child for its crying. Your visit is brief and to the point. You reassure and then you leave again. The child cries, and exactly ten minutes later you do it again.

Depending on the willpower of the infant, this could go on for hours — many hours. Eventually the infant will collapse, exhausted, and sleep, though some parents told of babies that woke up again later the same night, to repeat the whole performance. This was recounted with wide eyes, conveying all the horror of those movies when the terrifying zombie murderer, finally killed by the hero, magically revives at the end of the film, only to reappear in endless sequels. Mothers explained to me how they put on headphones, to drown out the pathetic wails. They presented a poignant picture of themselves huddled over a watch, headphones blasting, eyes fixed on the minute hand as it slowly crept around the dial. Fathers were more blasé, as if it were a mark of masculinity to be oblivious to infant screams. ·Mothers spoke of breasts surging with milk at the sound of the baby crying; the whole project was always described as a scene of intense emotional conflict. But they all agreed on one thing: the method works. After one night of this, or two, or three — no child had ever held out longer than a week, I was assured — after this treatment, the baby never wakes up in the night again.

They also all solemnly informed me that if you give in once, if you break down and get the baby out of bed and suckle it, or (heaven forbid) take it downstairs or into your bed, then you have to start all over again. You will have undone in a moment everything you have achieved in all those many hours of discipline and self-restraint, because the baby will once again believe that it can get what it wants. And you must start from scratch, obliterating that idea.

On the other hand, somewhat contradicting the infallibility of this process, real enthusiasts for Dr Ferber would talk about 'night wandering', and his recommendations for nipping that too in the bud. Night wandering is something that toddlers do, when they're old enough to sleep in a bed, and old enough to open doors. They wake up, and climb out of bed, and come and find you. They walk into your bedroom in the middle of the night. So you Ferberize the child again. This time their advice was as follows: you get the two-year-old back into its bedroom, and you close the door so the kid is on the inside and you're outside in the hall. You hang on to the doorknob with all your strength, thus preventing the (by now hysterical) child from opening the door. You simultaneously shout instructions through the door, telling the kid to get back into bed, promising that you will open the door when, and only when, the child is in bed again. One can imagine the sound-effects: the child screaming at the top of its lungs, the mother calmly shouting: 'Get into your bed, darling. Get into your bed, and then I'll open the door.' Throughout, the parent is keeping an eye on the time, because again every ten minutes you take a break, open the door, and have some form of eye to eye contact with the kid. Then, after a couple of minutes, you slam the door again, and repeat the whole scene. Again, the treatment (apparently) works. After a night or two (or three or four) of this, the child doesn't get out of bed in the night again.

My friend's boyfriend used to hit her four-year-old son as punishment for getting up at six a.m. and coming into their room. The child was told he must stay in his own bed in the morning. This led to a problem with bedwetting: the kid was too scared to get out of bed in the morning and go to the toilet. Wide awake, terrified, he would sit in his bed and pee.

But Ferberization isn't meant to be a punishment. It's simply a tried and true method of making the child sleep all night. I regarded it as a way to introduce the infant to despair. No point in crying for the parent, because the parent won't come. It's not that the parents are absent; they're there, in the house, but they won't come. That's what I think of as despair.

So I never did it. Not because I thought it really harmed the baby — I figure babies are unbelievably resilient, and can cope with almost anything. Although even avid Ferberizers disagreed on the best age to do it, some thinking the younger the better, others feeling under six months, or under eight months, or under ten months, was a bit extreme.

I didn't do it because I didn't have any wish to go through it myself. And my daughter still wakes in the night and calls out for me. She's two and a half. She comes into our room at ten past six every morning, and climbs into bed with us, to talk. After a while, she says, 'Get up. Get up. Breakfast time.' When she cries in the night, I go to her.

5. On weaning

Lacan talks about weaning, but he seems to be referring to the period from about six months when the baby starts getting more of its nourishment from solid food. So it's the transition to solids he's talking about, not necessarily the moment when the breast is taken away forever. Other analysts use the word weaning to refer to the daily withdrawal of the breast, an event that is continually repeated, when the mother removes her nipple from the baby's jaws. But in my book weaning is something else again, weaning is when you give up the breast completely. That's enough, that's it, no more. All gone.

When E. would cry in the night, I would give her the breast. She'd go to sleep again, sucking. This is not a good idea, because going to sleep by yourself is an extremely useful skill to acquire. E. would go to sleep in my arms, nipple in her mouth. I couldn't figure out any other way to get her to go to sleep. The whole thing flummoxed me.

With this approach to breastfeeding, weaning loomed large. I was anxious about it for months, unable to imagine how I would ever have the strength of mind to carry it out. And I didn't want to quit, anyway, because quitting meant acknowledging she wasn't a baby any more, and I knew I was likely to have only this one, and I didn't want to give it up, or to think about giving it up.

I kept imagining E. demanding the breast and me saying no, and not wanting to say no, and the whole scene being unspeakably painful for everyone. I kept imagining us both in tears, like lovers crying together after they've decided to split up. I imagined her crying, and me unable to refuse her. It wasn't like that, as it happened, probably because I'd left it for so long, maybe she was really more than ready to pack it in. And while I was immensely relieved, I was also a little sad, that it was so *very* easy to quit.

Things were complicated for me because E. never took anything from a bottle: not expressed breast milk, not formula, not water, juice, cow's milk, nothing. It was as if to say, you know very well that's not the breast, don't think you can fob me off with this crummy substitute, I'd rather hold out for the real thing.

She wasn't interested in substitutes for me, she never sucked her thumb, or became attached to a single 'transitional object' (the rag or the blankie or the teddy which theoretically represents the absent mother). E. drank juice from a cup with a spout, so thirst wasn't a problem, but if I gave her milk to drink, invariably she would simply open her mouth and let it pour out over her chin and chest. I left her all day, five days a week, at daycare, where she was very happy. And when we were together, she sucked as much as and whenever she wanted to — all night long. As if the fact that we were separated meant she got her required quota of intimate contact and sucking and nutrients between the hours of six p.m. and eight a.m., instead of during the day.

By the time I picked E. up at five-fifteen every day, my breasts would be bursting, and we'd drive home, and immediately settle down on the sofa for a nice long suck. Once, I was so uncomfortable that I sat in the car and breastfed her, just to get some relief. After that, she expected it every day, and would cry bitterly if I tried to put her in her car seat. It had never crossed her tiny mind that it was possible to suck before we got home to the sofa. But I made an exception, and once she knew it was possible, she insisted on it. So, for a month or six weeks, every day we sat in the car as the sun went down, breastfeeding, until I decided it really wouldn't do. It was the first major change that I made, the first time I refused her demand, but I explained why I was doing it, and then I just did it, I put her in her car seat and drove her home. In retrospect it seems laughable — at the time it was momentous. She was nine months old. It is possible to make adjustments, I thought, it is possible to say, not now. Not here, not now, no.

On the day after her first birthday, without consulting Robert, somewhat manically, I moved her out of our room (and our bed) into her own room (and her own bed) across the hall. (There was a little crib in our room, where she slept about half the night, but most of the time she was in bed with us, grazing at the breast.) Then I had to get out of bed at irregular intervals all night long, to go into her room to feed her. Then my term ended, and I was able to take some naps while E. was at daycare, and we cut down. We cut down to two feeds a day, one before bed, one upon waking in the morning. Again, we talked about it for a couple of weeks before I actually carried it out. Which means I talked about it, incessantly, a repetitious and reassuring monologue as we drove to and from daycare.

Cutting down was major, as we'd been breastfeeding at intervals of one to two hours from two a.m. on, and it wasn't easy, because she still woke up, and wanted something, but not a bottle, or a cup, or anything analogous to the breast. Luckily I'd discovered ice chips a couple of weeks before; she'd been vomiting and couldn't keep even breastmilk down, and Nina, my daycare provider, said, ice chips. It's a way to get liquid into them that isn't in the form of a drink. So during those first nights, I would stumble downstairs to the kitchen when E. woke up, and smash some ice in a teatowel with a hammer, and stagger back upstairs to the dark bedroom, where I would kneel by her bed and slide fragments of ice into her mouth. Needless to say, some pieces slipped down her neck into her pyjamas, undoing the overriding motivation of helping the child to go back to sleep. It was pretty ridiculous.

Eventually I decided we'd quit in October. I wasn't worried about her, it was clear she was probably ready to quit; it was me I was worried about. I had to decide on a deadline and then stick to it. We were travelling a lot, and everyone says don't try to wean your baby when you're on the move, so I waited until we'd been settled a month, and then we did it. I started talking about it on the 2nd of October, and we stopped the evening session without too much difficulty. It was easy to read her stories instead. The morning suck is universally acknowledged to be the hardest, however, and suddenly it was

October 21st and I'd decided the whole thing had to be over with by the end of the month. So I kept talking, about how we would still be close and hug and love each other, but we weren't going to do that sucking stuff any more, and I decided Friday morning would be the cut-off date.

All week I worried, imagining my tears on Thursday morning when she unwittingly had her very last breastfeed. What a picture, a Victorian sentimental painting: the ageing mother, head bowed as tears silently trickle down her nose to drop onto the reclining form of the suckling child, utterly unaware of her fate. It was not to be. By some quirk of providence, E. was ill on the Thursday morning, and showed no interest in breastfeeding. Thus we were both unaware that the very last breastfeed had indeed been the very last one. She seemed to have forgotten all about it on Friday, and Saturday, and to our amazement, didn't ask for the breast until Monday evening. Then I explained again, I said, 'Don't you remember? We're not going to do that any more.' Etc. She didn't seem to mind. So much for my tears, her tears, her tantrums, my ambivalence, the whole emotional mess.

5. Armenia

I went to Soviet Armenia in 1984; there was a museum of children's art in Yerevan. The guide explained that children are very important in Armenia, because of the massacres, the genocide. The air was very bad. Subsequently I read an article by Michael Arlen Jr., he described the boys in Armenia talking about Los Angeles, they say, 'I will drive a red BMW, when I get to Los.' I live in Los Angeles now, and occasionally I refer to the city as Los, hoping to start a trend. So far it hasn't had much impact.

In LA I meet Armenians in the body shops, the auto body repair shops. They have unbelievably bright blue eyes and amazing bone structures and easy to guess Armenian names. When I tell them I have been to Yerevan, they are perplexed: 'Why?' they say. They look at me with some contempt, as if I were too stupid to have figured out that's the place to leave, not a place to *go*.

I will drive a red BMW when I get to Los. Los(s) is where we live, and having a kid only brings this home more vividly. Birth is the first separation, it's the beginning of learning how to separate. And then it goes on and on.

I still have a big belly, since having E., and I finally recognized that it wasn't just because I hate lying on the floor, I hate sit-ups and crunches and all the other things you have to do. A shop assistant in Adolfo Dominguez said to me, 'Oh but you *have* to get rid of it during the first year, or else you never can.' This provided another excuse: if it was impossible to get rid of my maternal bulk, why bother to try? But the deeper reason was simply that I loved being pregnant, I loved taking up that space in the world, and knowing that a baby was in there. I wore black leggings and form-fitting Lycra zip jackets, very *Avengers*, which unerringly outlined my monumental shape. So I don't mind being big, I don't mind, even, if people think I might be pregnant. I haven't really given it up, that maternal position, that fecund body. I haven't bounced back. It's been more like a crawl, for me.

I'm beginning to think I'm almost ready, now, almost ready to leave this unlikely territory, the land of plenitude, where I've been living with E. I'm getting ready for Los(s), where mourning what has been and what will never be goes hand in hand with celebrating what I've got.

It's geographic, the maternal position, it's like living in another, parallel world. Having a baby is like going to a very particular place, and when you've had one, and you're thinking about having another, the question becomes, do I want to go back there? Is that really where I want to be? It's like going into exile, where you'll find other kindred spirits, and all sorts of secret knowledge, untold pleasures, yet your experience will be invisible, uncommunicable, and unacknowledged by the world outside.

I want to depart gracefully, now, I want to be able to give up this wish. It seems possible, for the first time, and I'm beginning almost to want to leave that odd world, the realm of mothers and infants, to let go of the perpetual longing and the multiple gratifications and even my maternal body. I'm waving my head from side to side, shaking my hands, letting go of the pain. I'm almost ready, and I want to come back.

Ghost Story

Night fell.

She said: Paper dolls can't sit down, they're inflexible, flat like a picture. You're just meant to dress them and undress them, you can make them talk but their clothes tend to fall off, those white flaps never hold the dress on if you make a paper doll do anything at all except stand there. For Christmas I got a Jackie Kennedy paper doll, and her wardrobe included the very same pale pink Chanel suit she was wearing on that fateful day in Dallas when the President was shot. There was even the pillbox hat, a little square of pink paper, with a slit in it, to slip over her black cardboard hair. She was smiling, that big smile, and her black hair curled around her face. One arm was part of the body, and one stretched out, so you could hang her handbag on it. Her legs weren't cut out, there was a white triangle of cardboard between them, and under her feet there was the crossed cardboard base that made her stand up. I cut the pink suit out, and put it on, carefully folding the white flaps around her flat shoulders, and then I decided to re-enact the assassination. Paper dolls can't sit down, so although I managed to find an appropriate-sized car in my brother's room, Jackie sat in it, or on it, at a terrible angle, completely stiff and unnatural. I borrowed Ken from Barbie (Ken for Kennedy I thought, and the hair was almost exactly the same). He was slightly too big, and of course his plastic three dimensionality threatened Jackie's precarious hold on identity, but then he was the President. I took my arithmetic and geography books, which were thick, and put them in a pile, to make the Texas Schoolbook Depository, overlooking the motorcade, and I stole a little plastic soldier, lying down pointing a rifle, to be Lee Harvey Oswald. He was much smaller than Jackie or Ken, but that was OK because he was in the distance, a tiny little person shooting a gun. (Then I remembered Jack Ruby shooting him on TV, that was much closer, but Jackie wasn't there when that happened, this was Jackie's big day.) I found my green sweater and made a grassy knoll, and then I played Assassination. My sister sat on the bed and watched. Bang!! I took my crayons and coloured in the red bloodstains on the pink Chanel suit, the one she wouldn't take off, the one she kept on, so that everyone could see the blood. Later I found some children paper dolls, to be Caroline and John-John, but they were almost as big as Jackie, so I gave up. The funeral was too difficult, I couldn't figure out how to dig a grave in the floor of my room, and anyway Jackie's wardrobe didn't have anything black.

He said : Widows do strange things sometimes. The woman who inherited the Winchester fortune, the fortune made from the Winchester 73 rifle, first her child died, and then her husband died, so she went to a medium, a clairvoyant, who said, you are being punished by the ghosts of all the thousands of people killed by the Winchester 73. The only way to protect yourself is to go as far away as possible, to California, and the only way to stop your house from being haunted is to make sure it is forever unfinished, forever being built, the sounds of the hammers must never stop. So she went out to San Jose, which was the middle of nowhere, and she built this huge useless house that was perpetually added to for thirty years, so that it makes no sense at all; she lived in it all alone, with builders endlessly working on it, money flowing, in continual payment, to keep it always unfinished. She didn't make plans, so the house is full of doors opening onto blank walls, or onto a drop of two storeys, and staircases that go nowhere, and chimneys without fireplaces (she believed that ghosts come down the chimney like Santa Claus so she built lots of false and deceptive ones) and stained glass and skylights and amazing internal windows and holes in the floors and walls so she could watch her servants, she was sure they were stealing from her, because she was very very rich, and kept getting richer, because of course the rifle business went on doing well. And eventually, after her death, Walt Disney heard about this house, this spooky house with its crazed architecture completely obsessed with ghosts, and it became the prototype for the famous Haunted House at Disneyland. Of course, Oswald used a Mannlicher Carcano.

She said : The Winchester 73 was the gun they used to wipe out the Indians; it would have been Indian ghosts whistling down the chimneys in San Jose. Up north in BC, the Kwakiutl Indians think that every human being is the ghost of a salmon, or a whale, or a bear. It's not as if this simple animal stands in for a complicated person, but the other way around, the salmon is the most complicated thing of all, and when you die, the ghost jumps into the seas and the rivers, becoming a salmon again. It's like everybody is a ghost, and ghosts are jumping in and out of things all the time, changing their form depending on the situation and the time of year. And of course salmon really are complicated, even scientists don't understand how they work, because you know they have to find their way back to the very lake where they were conceived and born, spawned, out of all those fish eggs, they find that lake, and do sex, and die. It's amazing. As if we had to find the house, the bed, the back seat of the Chevy, where we were conceived, in order to fuck just once, and die.

He said : I saw a salmon ladder once, where they've built a dam, so the salmon can't get back up the river, and so they build a sort of wooden stairway up the side of it, with water rushing down, and the fish battle their way up the ladder, leaping against the rushing water, struggling to get to their lake, to die.

She said : It seems like sort of a wasted effort. The Kwakiutl Indians used to do potlatch; each band would spend all winter saving up and making carved boxes for the fish grease, which was their most precious thing, and lovely canoes and costumes and totem poles and collecting heaps of blankets, and then they'd have a potlatch which was like a big party, and all this wealth would be destroyed. Originally it was given away to all the guests, and then later, when they were all getting richer and richer (because the Anglos were buying furs and paying for them with Hudson's Bay Company blankets, red and blue, so that the blankets became like money, a kind of currency, so many hundred blankets equals one carved canoe), later in a final decadent version of potlatch they would just put all the things in a great heap and burn it. It was to show what a mighty chief you were, the more you could throw away, the more powerful you were. They thought of it as vomiting up the ghosts of all the things inside you, the stuff you'd eaten up, or consumed.

He said : Sometimes I think all the stocks and shares are the ghosts of the workers who lived and died working for those companies, and the Financial Times Index is like a salmon ladder, this completely artificial and perverse thing, and the shares go leaping up it, up and up, and then suddenly they come crashing down, to wreak terrible revenge on the rich people, like the Winchester 73 rifle ghosts.

She said : Yes, and the ghosts of all the workers shriek with pleasure as the market slides, and there's death and destruction and sacrifice on all sides, in this great global potlatch, and the ghost of the Azzedine Alaia dress jumps into the American Express card, and the ghost of the Porsche jumps into the Filofax, and the ghost of the matte black bleeper jumps into the Cartier underwater watch, and everything is transmuted and transformed, and given away and destroyed and killed, in a great party at the lake at the end of the river!

He said : Can I have another mince pie?

Ghost Story

She said : Gifts come back to haunt you.

He said : Giving something away is a kind of assassination. And when you eat something you've destroyed it, it disappears.

She said : The only way not to be haunted is to never finish.

He said : Whenever it's Christmas in the movies you always know something terrible is going to happen.

She said : Scary.

The wind howled in the dark night, singing through the leafless trees.

MINITEL 3615

It was a love affair by electronics, a love affair by MINITEL, the Paris computer system that offers interactive communication between users, who type texts onto their computer screens, these texts transmitted instantly from monitor to monitor, through the telephone lines of the city. An abstract, immaterial love affair, therefore, a literary love affair, epistolary without the literal object, no pen, ink, or paper, only an ephemeral alphabet written in white light against a plain grey screen. The MINITEL system is low tech: you can book theatre tickets, or find out railway timetables, you can check your bank balance and then, you can give in, accept the invitation posed by incessant, all-pervasive advertising, and dial 3615, the number that lets you into the network of lovers, those who pursue sexual gratification through the exchange of texts, only. No kiss, no touch; no object: no letter, or scrap of silk; no image, no voice, even; no trace of the body. The body vanishes, leaving a flickering screen, rows of words inscribed in fugitive white light.

C : Hello. Edward?
E : You speak English? — or write English?
C : That's right.
E : Good. We can do it in English, then.
C : Excellent.
E : Begin.
C : How?
E : Any way you please.

C : Do you know the 3615 poster, the big one at the corner of rue Malher and rue St Antoine? The one of the very young girl, the girl with dark hair?
E : The one that's repeated all along the tunnels at the Bastille?

C : Yes. That's me. Catherine.

E : That's how I imagine you. A libertine child, the child who read James Bond at the age of seven, Fanny Hill at nine, and was deep in Philosophy in the Bedroom and Henry Miller at eleven.

C : But of course!

E : The intellectual, precocious, clever child, the voracious reader, sneaking these forbidden books off her parents' shelves. Your parents are absent, uninterested, preoccupied, and would possibly be amused, if they knew — until they discovered the extent of your depravity, how every afternoon after school you lounge, like those girls in Balthus paintings, your skirt falling back over your skinny thigh, book in hand, eyes racing, racing over the page, and then moving more slowly, desultory. Eleven years old, lying on the sofa — and already too old, corrupt, fascinated. Hooked. That's how I picture you, Catherine.

C : Yes.

E : The apartment was rather large; long rooms with windows opening onto narrow balconies, thin white light reflecting off pale stone, Paris light, reflecting back on the white walls of these rooms. There were paintings on these walls, and the parquet creaked in places. You remember — a specific set of sounds, the familiar sounds of different people moving through this space, these rooms and corridors. The woman who cooked and cleaned and kept an eye on you. Your mother with her luncheon appointments, her shopping, her endless telephoning. Your father so beautiful, with his dark hair falling across his forehead. Every day he shut himself into his study; he would eat his lunch off a tray that was left outside his room, in the corridor, and invariably he would walk for an hour after lunch, to clear his head, he said. You remember, perhaps, one afternoon when you got up from your nap, and walked down the corridor. You could hear Ariette singing quietly to herself, working in the kitchen. You wanted to ask your father the meaning of a word in a book you were reading. He was not in his study. You went to the bedroom, your parents' room. You looked through the keyhole, your dress falling forward as you bent down to look. Your legs were bare, and they began to shake slightly, as your heart pounded, watching your father fucking your mother. She was pale, naked, absolutely passive, flat — her arms were stretched wide, he held them out, flat, as his body moved over her. You saw, you understood, you wanted that — that precisely, to become him, to become her — to lie on a bed in the afternoon, the shutters drawn across the windows, a sense of the busy city traffic below, the white reflected light of Paris outside, autumn, and you, and Ariette, carrying on your normal afternoon, and here, in this shadowed room, this excess of passion enacting itself. As you watched, your mother didn't move, it was as if she were dead, but her mouth was open, a series of little 'Oh!'s came out of this mouth, and you felt your vagina flicker. This was what you wanted, precisely this.

C : Perhaps. Go on.

E : The next afternoon, you were alone, reading, as always. Your parents had gone to the country, to stay with friends, without you. Ariette was asleep, sound asleep, in her room. Taking a glass of apricot juice from the fridge, you'd looked in and seen her sleeping there. You were reading, and as you read you rocked back and forth gently in your chair, as was your habit. You sat with one pale, bare leg folded under you, your foot tucked under you, and rocked gently. Now you associate the flood of words in your mind, reading, that pressing flow, moving onward, reading this, now, with the rising pleasure, as you gently rocked back and forth. But the book was surprising: suddenly it described a scene of petticoats, white thighs, a thin leather riding whip across those thighs. Your fingers longed to touch yourself, you remember your mother lying flat, so thin and pale, her arms held outstretched, held down by the man with the beautiful body. She could not touch herself. You can. Reading the scene over and over, picturing the woman's pale legs, her skirts pulled up, the fine whip coming down, you put your hand under your skirt, down into your knickers, and slip your middle finger easily between those lips. With your other hand you stroke your mouth, leaning forward over the book, which lies flat on the table. You come. You think, as the rush recedes, you think, that is what I want. To be the thighs, the whip, the eyes, watching, the woman leaning over, who cannot see. The hand that holds the whip, the thighs that feel it. That is what I want.

C :

E : I'm still here.

C : Do you want to make a date?

E : Do you mean here, on the machine? Or in real life?

C : The machine is better than real life, don't you think? We could arrange the time, and meet.

E : Yes.

C : Every afternoon at half-past five, perhaps, a conversation in writing. An exchange, of some sort.

E : Not at the weekends.

C : All right.

E : I'm afraid I can't make it tomorrow. Wednesday.

C : Till then.

C : Edward?

E : Catherine.

C : Lassitude.

E : My theme for the day?

C : There should be a symbol on this thing for laughter, asterisks or something. Or maybe I should write it out, as they do in novels: she laughed.

E : There should be symbols for all the different bodily

responses. A sharp intake of breath. Heart beating faster. Biting the lower lip. Eyes closing.

C : She blushed. She began to shake.

E : You are lying in a pool of shadows, lying flat on your wide, low bed. There is yellowing sunlight outside, the curtains blow in the mild wind, shadows moving in irregular patterns across your body, over the bed. It is late afternoon. You know you will have to get up soon, to put your dress over your head, pull on stockings and slip your narrow bony feet into high heels, put on your makeup and go out — to stand like a tower, swaying slightly, holding the cold wet long glass of vodka and tonic. Yes?

C : Isn't this getting a little too Martini-ad-esque?

E : Is it the condensation on the drink you object to? Too slippery?

C : This is supposed to be Lassitude.

E : OK. You are lying naked, flat on your bed, knowing that soon you will be standing upright, swaying slightly, in your high heels, your lipstick marking the edge of your glass. The transformation, from your present position, prone, seems unbelievable, beyond your power. Yet you know, magically, it will take place. Your hand gently slides over your naked thigh.

C : My hand gently slides over the soft inner skin of my naked thigh.

E : You hear a sound in the flat, you know there are other people nearby, they could call out to you, disturb you. It's nearly time to get up, get dressed, but you lie there, in the evening light, stilled, suddenly, listening — one hand on your thigh, one fingering your nipple absently — listening to see if someone is approaching.

C : I don't want anyone to interrupt me, to interrupt my pleasure, my lassitude.

E : Your hand moves, and your fingers slip perfectly along your cunt. Your cunt is wet, there isn't enough time. You must come straight away.

C : I must come quickly, knowing —

E : Knowing they are watching?

C : They are watching me.

E : I am watching you.

C : Yes.

E : I raise my hand and I bring it down with a great slap on your white arse. You are lying on your front now, your fingers moving, arse high, and I hit you over and over, your white skin turns red.

C : I'm coming now, as you hit me, watching me come, hitting me.

E : Good.

C : Thank you.

E : Tell me what you're thinking.

C : I'm thinking about obsession and writing. Pornography, or written sex, sex writing, seems to be made up of a series of clichés, endlessly banal. What we agree to do here, our implicit contract, is to submit to the clichés of the other. I give in to you, I accept whatever you designate as sexy — or erotic — or whatever you want to call it. These elegant little cuts and blows.

E : Yet no marks remain, no bruises, or scars.

C : True. I suspect my pleasure lies in the knowledge that we are invisible to each other; it amuses me, the endless permutations of this relation. A woman possibly, or an old man, you can write to me as if you were a desperate teenager, maybe, or an eleven-year-old girl.

E : Or none of these.

C : The public images sustain us, in the background — more clichés of pleasure. As we walk down the street, on everyday errands, we can't not take in the erotic billboards and posters that the phone company so thoughtfully provides, enticing us back to the machine.

E : I see you every day, Catherine, in the Metro — your gigantic shoulder, your flawless skin, seduce me.

C : We can pretend whatever we like, flawless skin, unlimited wealth — huge flats with creaking parquet, mottled mirrors over the marble fireplace, some image of Paris derived from a grotesque hybrid of sixties movies and Atget photographs — when in truth (maybe) we can't pay the fucking phone bill, with this terrible MINITEL amount stuck on the end. I've stopped going out, lately, making some crazed economy that an evening at the MINITEL monitor is cheaper than an evening out. Compulsion?

E : Obsession. I find that I've begun to like writing, for the first time. The writing disappears. There is no copy, no original. This writing (like no other) is pure gift.

C : For me everyday life has become charged with sexual possibility: the young man in the butcher's, the fishmonger, the woman behind the bar, the man taking tickets — I've made it with any one of them, or none, or all. Who knows? No one knows. I think we'll have to stop, soon.

E : Why?

C : This could get dodgy, don't you think?

E : What?

C : All this reading and writing.

E : I've been reading this book about Greek lyric poetry, Sappho, which claims there's a connection between desire — or the possibility of writing about desire — and the invention of the Greek alphabet. Because apparently the Greek alphabet was the first to have consonants, and this is crucial because consonants are abstract — they cannot be spoken without a vowel, like T is spoken 'tea', etc, etc. Which means that writing T itself, alone, is a radical break with the previous, oral culture.

C : Oh.

E : Shall I go on?

C : Don't stop.

E : Consonants mark the edge of a sound, or a word. And since desire is all about representing what's absent — since desire is about edges, because the child discovers the difference between itself and the world by encountering edges that it wishes didn't exist — so consonants are crucial to the writing of desire. So Sappho is possible, supposedly.

C : I always think consonants are penises and vowels are vaginas. And a comma is like a clitoris, and a dash is like a prick.

E : I want to meet you, Catherine.

C : Never. Over and out.

C : Begin, Edward. We'll take turns, today.

E : She knelt down to suck his prick.

C : They were travelling on a train.

E : The floor was dirty; the train rocked as dull green fields rolled by: England.

C : She undid his flies, and looked at his prick, poking out; the naked skin, a sudden contrast against the woollen fabric of his trousers, the coarse material of the railway seats.

E : The inside lining of his overcoat was shiny pale grey satin; she rubbed this against his prick.

C : Her knees were beginning to hurt; she stood up and raised her skirt, slightly.

E : He put his hand under her skirt, he felt the silk of her slip smooth against her legs, he felt the edge of her stocking, the tight elastic garter, he felt her naked wet cunt.

C : His hand touched her clitoris, and moved back to find the opening of her vagina.

E : She raised her right leg, placing her foot on the seat beside him, and moved closer, lowering herself over his prick.

C : His hand was holding her pale arse, under her skirts, guiding her onto his prick, while with the other he fingered and pinched her small breast through the thin fabric of her dress.

E : Kicking off her black high heels, she clambered over him, her arms around his neck, beginning to fuck him.

C : As she moved slowly up and down, her tight wet cunt

sucking his prick, her clitoris brushed against his trousers, touched the cold metal of his belt buckle.

E : He looked out of the window, amazed at the oblivious world passing by. It crossed his mind the train might arrive at a station, someone could get in.

C : Holding his head in her hands, she bit his lip, looking into his eyes. She said, I want you to come.

E : I want you to come.

C : Come now, she said, moving faster, the buckle clicking against her clitoris, hard prick inside her, coming.

E : Now.

C : Yes.

E : Now.

C : Yes.

E : Now.

E : Tell me about sex in cars.

C : I don't think I'm in the mood.

E : Mood?

C : Moving cars or parked cars?

E : As you like.

C : We met in the street. We were very young — city hippies. People always think of that time as all about geodesic domes in Arizona and health food, nature, you know, but really hippies were street people, city streets, hanging out, smoking, doing drugs, passing the time. Anyway we met on the street — he was leaning against a car, smoking a joint, and he smiled and offered it to me. So I leaned up against this car beside him, very cool, and we talked, obliquely, easily. He was giving me the eye, he had a wild, sexy look, crazy smile — classic ex-junky's bad teeth — and you know, I was happy, I was laughing with him, it was fine. Very quickly it became clear what we wanted. It was maybe nine at night; the sky was dark but the streets were wild, a hot night on the North Side, lots of people on the street, cars slowly moving by. We got into that car and started to make out. In retrospect it strikes me that maybe he could have driven me somewhere, if it was his car, but probably I've forgotten, maybe he was waiting for somebody, his friend . . . I don't know. What I remember, what I remember is pulling my tampax out, opening the car door and dropping it there in the gutter, so that we could fuck. That's sex in parked cars.

E : I have to admit I didn't find that account very erotic. More of sociological interest.

C : I'm struck by the amazing urgency of it, we had to have it, had to do it. Sexual momentum. And of course the extraordinary discomfort of fucking in that car, our physical contortions to get his prick into my vagina — and then the secondary, peripheral sense of people passing by on the street, the lights, cars . . . It was dark in the back seat, and hot, the car windows were half open, we were trying not to make too much noise. We were all breathless and laughing when we were through, and I remember pulling myself together, finding my underpants and pulling them up, and stepping out of the car, onto the busy sidewalk again, my body flushed with excitement. We never saw each other again.

E : It sounds like an inversion of Baudelaire — instead of the flâneur who sees the woman of his dreams and loses her forever, walking through the crowded city streets, you find each other, fuck, and say goodbye.

C : That's right. Immediate gratification, simply. Not like this.

E : How's it going?

C : There's something so strange about sitting down to this little monitor, little monster, text producer, this machine. It's like an altar in my house — it reminds me of a Nichiren Buddhist altar; my friend used to chant before hers, every day. And every day now I come to my little MINITEL altar, every day at the same time, I kneel down, to read your written words, to direct my pleasure.

E : To submit.

C : It seems so exposed — are others listening in, despite these closed lines, closed doors . . . What about the technicians, the phone company itself?

E : Others like us.

C : This weird combination of exhibitionism and anonymity. You can never find me.

E : Yet I know your secrets, I know what makes you come.

C : You know, and therefore everyone knows. Anyone.

E : You would like to be truly exposed, to an audience — to see yourself being seen.

C : No. That's what is so perfect about this machine. Alone, I can imagine your look, your knowing invasion of my control, my privacy, my autonomy — I can give in to it, ashamed of myself, this shuddering exposure. Your look turns my careful world inside out, peels away my skin. My cunt flowers, reaching out. I crouch here in the darkness, these winter afternoons, scanning your words, entirely alone, invisible, and yet entirely exposed — to you, dear reader.

E : Dear?

C : Dear stranger. You have become dear to me, since you get it right.

E : And the others?

C : Others?

E : Who get it right, or wrong.

C : You imagine me glued to this magic box all day? All night?

E : No.

C : Sometimes late at night when I'm alone I wake up and listen in, play the field. I take my chances, as they say, and once in a while I come across congenial types. Other times I am bored, simply, and continue only out of politeness. Occasionally I'll do a party but it always seems that everything's happening at once, it's hard to keep things focussed.

E : You and I are good at taking turns.

C : Which do you like better, transmitting or receiving?

E : I like giving you pleasure. Your orgasm confirms my power, it is always infinitely surprising to me. The idea of your excitement makes me extremely excited.

C : Maybe it's the machine itself we like, really. Detachment.

E : Sometimes I like to listen in to an exchange, where the lines have been left open. I like to listen without making my presence known, like watching through a keyhole.

C : There, it's just power again. That's what you get off on.

E : Let's leave the lines open, and see how much you like the notion of a silent listener, or reader, I should say.

C : Someone watching me. Perhaps.

E : Yes, next time. I insist.

C : There are men on the scaffolding across the street, working. They look at me, they can see me, here.

E : The man sees you reading, reading with your hand between your legs, he knows you want him to watch. You pretend you don't know he is watching you. His hand touches his prick, hard in his loose trousers. You continue to move your fingers, sinking them into your wet swollen cunt.

C : I pretend someone is watching me. I pretend you are about to walk in, surprise me, punish me, fuck me.

E : I will fuck you until you cry out to stop . . .

C : Yes.

E : Now.

C : Yes. Stop.

C : This whole process is in some ways so reminiscent of the couch — with the difference that you respond, so to speak, while the analyst could not. I imagine that you know everything anyway, already. Possibly the analyst knew everything too, but couldn't show it, couldn't let himself show it off.

E : This is nothing but showing off, this machine, turning towards an imaginary audience . . .

C : I feel so completely vulnerable, now, suddenly, and you seem so impenetrable, opaque. A blank wall, one-way mirror, mechanical camera, hidden eye . . .

E : Click, click, click. It was the clicking of her clitoris, wasn't it?

C : That's right. I didn't know you knew about that.

E : No dirty stories today?

C : I want to give you a text I found, I like it very much. It's very amusing. It's from a book about Leopold von Sacher-Masoch. I'll type it in, tomorrow.

E : Like jazz, you can type in a text, and then we can play variations on it.

C : Or free associate off it.

E : The talking cure, or in this case, the typing cure.

C : In which case you're the analyst?

E : I'm the object of desire, sweetness, surely.

C : There's a line in Fanny Burney, my favourite: 'You have been, as you always are,' he said, twisting his whip with his fingers, 'all sweetness.'

E : Not bad. Naked on her hands and knees she whimpered with mingled pain and excitement, her mouth dry, as he slowly brought the leather riding whip across her pale thighs, making shocking pink lines across her white skin. She knew he would fuck her, she was waiting — wanting it to go on forever, timeless, this combination of bright pain and blissful anticipation. With his whip he gently touched her wet cunt. He held his prick in his hand. She was shuddering, wanting to touch him, to touch herself — he forbade her to move. He reached to pinch her nipple hard, and moving suddenly, he fucked her up her tight arse, his hand grabbing her cunt, reaching greedily inside her.

C : She cried out with acute pleasure.

E : Now.

C : Now.

E : Thank you.

C : À demain. Over and out.

C : It's a contract he drew up with his lover in 1869.

E : OK.

C : One: Herr L. von Sacher-Masoch gives his word of honour to Frau Pistor to become her slave and to comply unreservedly for six months with every one of her desires and commands.

Two: For her part Frau Pistor is not to exact from him the performance of any action contrary to honour, i.e. which would dishonour him as a man or as a citizen. She is also to allow him to devote six hours a day to his professional work and agrees never to read either his correspondence or his literary compositions.

Three: The Mistress (Fanny Pistor) has the right to punish her Slave (L. von S-M) in any way she thinks fit for all errors, carelessness or crimes of lèse-majesté on his part.

Four: In short her subject, Gregor, must accord his mistress a wholly servile obedience and accept as an exquisite condescension any favourable treatment she may extend to him. He recognizes that he has no claim upon her love and he renounces all rights whatsoever to a lover's privileges.

Five: Fanny Pistor, on her side, promises to wear furs as often as possible, especially when she is in a cruel mood.

Six: This period of servitude is to be considered at an end after six months and no serious allusion to it will be permitted at the expiration of the period.

Seven: Everything which may have happened must be forgotten. The original love-relationship will then be resumed.

Eight: These six months need not run continuously. They may be interrupted for long periods, which will begin and end whenever the Mistress chooses. This pact is hereby put into force by the signatures of the contracting parties.

Commencing date 8 December 1869.

Signed: Fanny Pistor Bogdanoff

Leopold, Chevalier von Sacher-Masoch.

E : It's wonderful. I love the way she's not allowed to read a word he writes.

C : It was all about her, his writing.

E : And furs.

C : Especially in a cruel mood.

E : Basically she agrees to abuse him, within strict limits, set by him.

C : Those limits are counterbalanced, almost, I think, by the fact that she's the one who decides when to play this game, and when to stop playing.

E : I also like the way they're never allowed to allude to the six months, seriously, once it's over — as if they were only allowed to make jokes about it?

C : I think Fanny managed to extend the contract over a period of two or three years.

E : Wow.

C : I'm going to stop this soon.

E : When?

C : Next week.

E : We should make a new contract, like this one you've seduced me with.

C : If I have nothing more to do with you, I can pretend it never happened.

E : And the machine?

C : Send it back!

E : I don't believe you. I think I'm falling in love with you.

C : You've got to be joking. Over and out.

E : Tell me a story, Catherine.

C : I'm bored with stories.

E : Bored with solitary sex, with the machine, or with me?

C : When you write lines like that, I lose enthusiasm for all three.

E : Let's begin again. Describe yourself to me.

C : Ah, the appeal to narcissism. I'll tell you the truth, perhaps, this time. I am five foot three, with very thin, almost transparent skin and dark hair. I am wearing a black slip, appropriately, and I am sitting at a rather primitive computer screen. I have always wanted to look like Louise Brooks, but in fact I tend to look more like Bette Davis. I have wide round eyes, a bit buggy, and a pointed chin. I would like to have long, narrow eyes. I would like to be at least three inches taller. Some days I would like to be a man. However, I am older, these days, than I was, and I am beginning to accept my height, my buggy eyes, my femininity, and even my obsessive, repetitive, compulsive and dubious attachment to electronic pornographic exchange.

E : Let me tell you what you like.

C : No, let me tell you. You like to think about children, you like to think of children being beaten and children doing sex alone, fearful of being caught, found out. For you the beatings and the secret sex are part of the same thing, they go together. You take up the position of spectator — punitive, controlling — in defence against your deeper identification with the punished child. You project all these elements on to me: the thrill of forbidden mastur-bation, the longing to be caught, seen, looked at, the combination of innocence and depravity, the pleasure in punishment itself. This allows you to simply look on, passive, while I . . .

E : While you come, my love, tied up, whipped, prick in your mouth, your cunt, your breasts bruised, deliberately, deliberately, I make you cry out to be allowed to come, to be released.

C : Yes.

E : Now, do it.

C : Now.

E : Now, I'm watching.

C : Yes.

E : Yes.

C : Goodbye, Edward.

E : Until Monday?

C : Monday, yes.

C : What I've come to understand is that this machine has provided a space where the ambivalence that tears me apart is almost tolerable, only just bearable, within this highly artificial, totally isolated space of writing.

E : But, it seems, only if you know I can never find you out.

C : You were the faceless voyeur, I was the one doing sex, no? I was the object of desire, not you.

E : I find your use of the past tense excruciatingly painful.

C : There has to be a limit to this.

E : I cannot force you, I can only invite you to submit. I know it will please you.

C : Tell me once again.

E : I can refuse you also.

C : Once again.

E : You are at home, alone. The man you live with is away for a few days. You don't want to see anyone; you've left the answering machine on. Let them think you've gone away too. The days stretching empty before you, you know you can do whatever you please, alone in your shadowy flat, sleep as long as you like, read novels all afternoon. You take a bath at nine o'clock at night, and then stay up, listening to jazz and looking through old papers. You find a bunch of letters from a woman you seldom think about. You remember what it was like, the first time, in bed with her. She had thick, heavy red hair, that fell around her narrow face, dead white, and the softest skin you ever touched. You remember the transformation, how complete it was, like magic. She was a friend, an acquaintance,

209

years ago; you went round to see her, then, for tea; you smoked some dope, fell into her low bed. She became the most beautiful woman in the world. You remember how she put you down, how she told you she really wasn't into going to bed with straight women — as you melted, dazed by the creamy softness of her long body. Her hand on your cunt, wet kisses so sweet, she made you come over and over again. Remembering, you sense again those soft long arms, long thighs circling yours, you see her neck thrown back as you bite her breast, fierce suddenly. She laughs. You want her to come too. You touch her there where you like to be touched, and eventually she comes. Now, your lips are wet, your hand moves to touch your mouth, remembering.

C : Yes.

E : You powder your face, dead white, standing in front of the mirror; you put on your black coat, and go out. It's late, dark streets wet with rain, and the smell of oil on the city street as you cross. There's not much traffic. You walk down the wide street, knowing you'll be taken for a prostitute, knowing you're wearing a slip and nothing else under your coat. In the all-night coffee shop, there is a young woman sitting alone, reading the paper. You look at her, you ask if you can sit down. She nods briefly. You do not speak, but glance up, occasionally. Each catches the other looking, and you like her intelligent eyes, her blonde hair. At length you leave the café. She follows you. You wait in the dark street. She pauses, then she walks up to you. You are taller than her, you incline your head, slightly. You kiss her, on the lips, in the dark street.

C : And I take her home, into my bed, my soft sheets, I stroke her all over, I brush her hair, my sweet doll, my baby, my darling, I give her everything she wants, I never say a word.

E : No words.

C : That's what I want.

E : Let me be silent, then.

C : Goodbye, my dear.

E : Behind the figure of the punitive father, the man you imagine me to be, the man with the leather riding whip, lies the punitive mother, the woman who forbids, refuses. The man watching you, the man in control is a shadow figure. It is Mama who subdues, who gives and withholds your pleasure.

C : I know, I know all this, too well.

E : I will never hurt you, my love, I will only cause you the most pleasurable pain. I will give you everything you want.

C : Why do you say this? Why? I can't bear it.

E : You said you loved the idea that we both could be anyone we liked, the machine allowing infinite permutations of desire. I don't want to stop. I want to go on meeting you.

C : Desire is about the limits, the edges of things, endings of one kind or another. What's not there, what you can't have, haven't got. Obsession, this obsession is only a denial of those edges, endings, as repetition insists, persists, preventing possibilities of something else, something different. I want you to let go of me, stop looking at me, now.

E : Too many words. I've touched you. I want to go on and on, pleasing you.

C : I don't want to play any more, I've had enough. I want you too much, or this, and now it's become precisely what I want, I have no choice, I have to give you up. It.

E : You repudiate your own desire, you undo love.

C : This isn't love. This is a fantasy exchange. It can't go on, you know, it's too easy for me to see you as utterly undesirable, the sadistic man, cheating on everybody, endless lies, somehow manipulating my fantasies until they coincide, until they intersect with yours. It's like fucking in the back seat — prick into cunt, it's exciting, but it's so contorted, uncomfortable, it's not something you want to repeat, indefinitely. I'm uneasy. I've had enough of this. I don't want your stories any more.

E : Safe sex, darling, it's only words, writing. We cannot hurt each other, there's nothing there, no residue, it melts like snow, this writing.

C : No.

E : You can have whatever you want, no kiss, no touch, I will give you anything you want.

C : It's too dangerous, this, wanting this, and you know, for me, really, to tell the truth, it's not dangerous enough. I want more — or less, maybe, not this.

E : Then let's begin again. I will meet you tonight, Catherine, at that café, I will meet you at eleven tonight at that bar near the corner of the rue Malher and rue St Antoine. It's the one on the left, as you go up rue Malher, not very far, maybe one hundred metres, the little bar, on the left. Opposite the Hôtel Carnavalet. There's a pinball machine in the window. You won't have any trouble. I'll meet you there at eleven, tonight.

C : How would you recognise me?

E : You'll have short blonde hair, a pale raincoat, black boots.

C : I don't know what you mean. Is this a date on the machine or in real life?

E : I will find you easily in the crowded, noisy bar. I can see you, sitting in the dark at the back, the glass you are holding gleams in the dim light; you are waiting.

C : Don't you see I can't look at you.

E : I will blindfold you, my love.

C :

E : Then you will be entirely naked, only the silk scarf tied over your eyes.

C : No. No more words. Over and out.

Some Notes on Psychoanalysis
and Writing

Draft J. Mrs P. J. (age 27)

She had been married for three months. Her husband, a travelling salesman, had had to leave her a few weeks after their marriage and had been away for weeks on end. She missed him very much and longed for him. She had been a singer, or at any rate had been trained as one. To pass the time she was sitting at the piano singing, when suddenly she felt sick in her abdomen and stomach, her head swam, she had feelings of oppression and anxiety and cardiac paraesthesias; she thought she was going mad. A moment later it occurred to her that she had eaten eggs and mushrooms that morning, so she thought she had been poisoned. However, the condition quickly passed. Next day the maidservant told her that a woman living in the same house had gone mad. From that time on she was never free of the obsession, accompanied by anxiety, that she too was going to go mad.[1]

1. Interpretation

This exemplary text seems to walk a razor's edge between comedy and tragedy. So deadpan as to be virtually opaque, it cries out for interpretation. We read it ironically, no doubt, although Freud, writing somewhere around 1895, doesn't seem to see the joke. In a sense it's a pre-Freudian text. We're smiling as soon as we see the words 'travelling salesman'; we can guess what's coming next. Since it's a case history, the punchline is: she thought she (too) was going to go mad. A text like this foregrounds the work the reader is doing, the work of interpretation. It insists on the objectification of Mrs P. J. (age 27), and yet there is a way in which we identify with her. Certain elements invoke the gothic: the seemingly malevolent maidservant, the imaginary double in the form of her predecessor, the woman who went mad. 'Draft J' seems very contemporary in this combination of literary effects: generating a self-consciously ironic reading, insisting on the necessity for interpretation, it simultaneously makes us want to shriek with a kind of pained laughter.

2. Character

At a deeper level, 'Draft J' reveals a preoccupation with subjectivity, rather than character. It is closer in tone to the stage directions of nineteenth-century melodrama, than to the nineteenth-century novel; the inevitable work of interpretation will cast light less on the character of Mrs P. J. (age 27), than it does on the workings of the mind. (This is one reason why the text seems funny: Mrs P. J. is only a pretext, so to speak, for the text itself, the hysterical scene.) The case histories are useful to us writing now, partly because we're no longer interested in writing character, in the tradition of literary realism. In a sense, this text is impersonal; the symptomatic scene is presented as an object of study, or interrogation. The text separates off from its 'subject' (Mrs P. J.); it is autonomous and generative of meaning quite apart from any insight into her as a character. The text is emphatically an object (like the mind is an object); it is impersonal while *at the same time* dealing with subjectivity.

3. Subjectivity

Writing fiction now, the concept of 'character' goes out the window, to be replaced by a disparate collection of bodily sensations, part objects, speeches, anecdotes, writings, symptoms — evidence to construct the pathology that is identity,

the always incomplete, always being constructed and recon-
structed site of subjectivity.

4. Detail

From Freud we also take the critical importance of detail. In
'Draft J', it is the trivial detail of the eggs and mushrooms that
fixes the text, like a photograph is 'fixed' in the darkroom. Or
possibly the detail of the eggs and mushrooms is more like
Barthes's *punctum*,[2] the seemingly unnecessary, excessive detail
that both pierces the photographic image and pins it down.
Writing now, it is through the precise accumulation of such
exact details that we present the evidence, insisting on the
terrible specificity of psychic experience.

5. Lists

Narrative structure is foregrounded, as we tell our stories or
anecdotes with the same kind of self-consciousness that Freud
employed in the case histories, where he recounts the tracking
down of unconscious meanings in the virtual form of a detective
story. Stories become evidence, material to be worked on, or
with, to be incorporated into the analysis. These 'stories' are
juxtaposed with other kinds of ordering of experience: lists,
fragments, or free associations, placed together in what Yvonne
Rainer called a 'structure of accretion',[3] in which the piling up
of disparate parts makes complicated and contradictory sense of
things.

6. Language

Freud's text includes another kind of detail, the technical detail, viz. 'cardiac paraesthesias'. His sentence juxtaposes the phrase 'her head swam', Mrs P. J.'s point of view, with 'cardiac paraesthesias', Freud's retrospective diagnosis, addressed to his medical colleague, Fliess. The *Collins English Dictionary* (1986) defines paraesthesia as 'an abnormal or inappropriate sensation in an organ, part, or area of the skin, as of burning, prickling, tingling, etc.' The interruption of melodramatic anecdote by medical terminology shifts the text once again, from interior to exterior, from the personal to the apparently objective. Diagnostic detail (cardiac paraesthesias) collides with the detail of everyday life (eggs and mushrooms), generating a discursive tension. Embedded within the language of anecdote, we find the language of pathology, which itself stands next to the language of personal crisis. The text demonstrates ways in which these different vocabularies could be used against each other, so to speak, to propose an implicit critique of the assumptions and identifications of each.

7. Over-determination

Treating one's own or an invented history as a case history can itself be seen as a symptomatic act, an attempt to replace the (lost) analyst with one's very own pen. The pathos of this doomed attempt invites a further level of symptomatic reading. Writing fiction, I rely on the power of the Unconscious to make sense without my knowledge, to draw connections, create rhymes and rhythms, to speak *through* my text, despite, and also because of, my absolutely rigorous control of language.

8. Elsewheres

Realism posits a relation between text and referent, a mapping of description onto actuality in such a way that they can be measured against each other, they match. I have found that I write remembered places, elsewheres; I write London in Los Angeles, and New York in London, using the inevitable breaks and gaps of recollection to speak the patterns of subjectivity, to map an imaginary city. It is a remembered (i.e. a partially forgotten) London, a coded London (street names, as markers or stage directions, take the place of description), or a fantasized London — never the city itself. Like the notion of character, land- and cityscape lose value, unless as a presentation of psychic reality: memory, fantasy, or loss.

9. Palimpsest

There is no time in the Unconscious.[4] The literary strategies of superimposition and juxtaposition that we employ allow us to place disparate elements together, regardless of temporal constraint, or sequences of cause and effect. The endless analytic process of re-writing, or re-working the past is itself inscribed in the text, where the same ground is gone over and over, using repetition with slight differences to convey the layering, the complex texture of psychic reality.

10. First person

We tend to write 'I', 'she', 'you', with a difference, to make plain the way in which the Unconscious makes objects of us all. '*Je est un autre.*'[5] By constantly shifting between I, she, you, we insist on instability, on the construction of subjectivity within an overlapping series of projections and identifications.

11. Second person

While the 'character' within the text is broken into pieces, parts of stories, recollections, the 'reader', unsettled by the careful use of the word 'you', is thrown out of place also. In this writing, as we move between first, second and third person, we are pushing against the limits of grammatical structure to shift, to de-centre the reader's imaginary identity, to challenge that fantasized wholeness.

12. Third person

It may be the voice of authority, the third person narration which seems to exclude both the writer and the reader from the text, but at the same time, it is also 'it', the Unconscious, the inevitable disruption of that authority. Finally it is the conditions, the terms within which we write: the irreducible and intransigent constraints of language.

13. Sex

When I am blocked, I read Freud. This is because I am interested in sexuality and language, and that is what psycho-analysis is all about. As Luisa Valenzuela said, Freud was 'my main porno book, psychoanalysis was how I found out about sex'.[6] I would put it slightly differently: psychoanalysis was how I found out about writing!

14. Dreamwork

Throughout this piece I have moved, somewhat awkwardly, between 'I' and 'we', as if I were writing about a group, however amorphous, of women writers (and artists) who might have some of these concerns in common. It's hard for me to tell how much this hypothetical group is a fantasy of my own, or how much more appropriate it might have been simply to refer to myself, my own writing project, throughout these notes. Yet I *want* to write 'we', it's an almost utopian act, the expression of a wish. To write 'we' implies that there may be many other women, mostly unknown to me, whose writing comes out of a conjunction of feminism, psychoanalysis, and theoretical work. (It's possible to think of this 'conjunction', in this context, as part of a specific historical moment, though not necessarily confined to it.) To a great extent, this is the imagined context within which my work is produced: it is the audience to whom my work is primarily addressed; most importantly, this is the writing I want to read. I envisage it as part of a larger process, the convergence of theoretical ideas and art practice in film, visual arts, performance, dance, video. I hope these notes help to sketch in some of the ways we can think about how that convergence takes shape in writing.

Notes

1 Freud, Sigmund, *The Complete Letters of Sigmund Freud to Wilhelm Fliess 1887–1904* (translated and edited by Jeffrey Moussaieff Masson, Cambridge and London, 1985), pp. 155–6.
2 Roland Barthes, *Camera Lucida* (1980) (translated by Richard Howard, London, 1984).
3 Cf. Yvonne Rainer, *Work 1961–73* (Halifax, Nova Scotia and New York, 1974), and Yvonne Rainer, *The Films of Yvonne Rainer* (Bloomington, Indiana, 1989).
4 Cf. 'The processes of the system Ucs are timeless; i.e. they are not ordered temporally, are not altered by the passage of time, in fact bear no relation to time at all.' Sigmund Freud, 'The Unconscious' (1915), *Collected Papers*, Vol. IV (London, 1934).
5 Rimbaud, as quoted by Anna Karina in Jean-Luc Godard's *Vivre Sa Vie* (1962), Tableau 4, The Police, Nana's interrogation. Literal translation: 'I is an other'.
6 Luisa Valenzuela, interviewed by Leslie Dick, *Fiction*, August 1988, p. 5.

Acknowledgements

These stories would not have been written without the support and participation of many people. I would first like to sincerely thank those friends who commissioned, edited and published them, in various forms:

Peter Ayrton, John X. Berger, Lesley Bryce, Helen Carr, Paul Dreniw, Max Eilenberg, Alison Fell, Leigh Haber, Dewi Lewis, Brian Massumi, Jane Mills, Olivier Richon, Mandy Rose, Marsha Rowe, Rodney Sappington, Amy Scholder, Tyler Stallings, Shelley Wanger.

Other friends also gave me encouragement and many different kinds of help, for which I remain eternally grateful:

Kathy Acker, Mark Ainley, Nancy Barton, Michael Bracewell, Sarah Chalfant, Alexander Cockburn, Caroline Evans, Amy Gerstler, Harriett Gilbert, Antony Harwood, Memory Holloway, Thomas A. Levin, M. Mark, Francette Pacteau, Sarah Parker, Anita Phillips, Kate Pullinger, Elizabeth Pulsinelli, Alison Richmond, Michèle Roberts, Terrel Seltzer, Ira Silverberg, Lesley Stern, Drake Stutesman, Betsy Sussler, Emma Tennant, Minna Thornton, Lynne Tillman, Michael Webb, Jane Weinstock, Benjamin Weissman and, last but not least, Peter Wollen.

Credits

'The Skull of Charlotte Corday' first appeared in *Other Than Itself: Writing Photography*, eds. John X. Berger and Olivier Richon (Manchester, 1989) and subsequently in *The Politics of Everyday Fear*, ed. Brian Massumi (Minneapolis, 1993)

'Generosity' first appeared in *The Seven Cardinal Virtues*, ed. Alison Fell (London, 1990)

'Envy' first appeared in *The Seven Deadly Sins,* ed. Alison Fell (London, 1988)

'Dysplasia' first appeared in *Serious Hysterics,* ed. Alison Fell (London, 1992)

'On Splitting: A Symptomatology' first appeared in *Uncontrollable Bodies: Testimonies of Identity and Culture,* eds. Rodney Sappington and Tyler Stallings (Seattle, 1994)

'MINITEL 3615' first appeared in *Sex and the City: A Serpent's Tail Compilation,* ed. Marsha Rowe (London, 1989) and subsequently in *Emergency* (London, 1990)

'Ghost Story' first appeared in *National Student Magazine* (London, 1987) and subsequently in *City Lights Review: Number 2* (San Francisco, 1988)

'Some Notes on Psychoanalysis and Writing" first appeared (as 'Notes on Freud and Writing') in *Women: A Cultural Review,* ed. Helen Carr (Oxford, 1990)

About the author

Leslie Dick was born in the United States in 1954. She lived in London from 1965 and now divides her time between London and Los Angeles, where she teaches in the art program at the California Institute of the Arts. Her short stories have been published in several anthologies and her first novel, *Without Falling*, was published in 1987. Her second, *Kicking*, was published by Secker in 1992.